W9-AYQ-252

LITTLE,
BROWN

1837

LARGE
PRINT

Also by James Patterson:

The Thomas Berryman Number
Season of the Machete
See How They Run
The Midnight Club
Along Came a Spider
Kiss the Girls
Hide & Seek
Jack & Jill
Miracle on the 17th Green
   (with Peter de Jonge)
Cat & Mouse
When the Wind Blows
Pop Goes the Weasel
Black Friday
Cradle and All
Roses Are Red
1st to Die
Suzanne's Diary for Nicholas
Violets Are Blue
2nd Chance (with Andrew Gross)
The Beach House (with Peter de Jonge)
Four Blind Mice
The Jester (with Andrew Gross)
The Lake House
The Big Bad Wolf
3rd Degree (with Andrew Gross)

Sam's Letters to Jennifer

A NOVEL BY

James Patterson

LITTLE, BROWN AND COMPANY

LARGE LB 1837 PRINT

3 1489 00504 2257

Copyright © 2004 by James Patterson

All rights reserved. No part of this book may be
reproduced in any form or by any electronic or
mechanical means, including information storage and
retrieval systems, without permission in writing from the
publisher, except by a reviewer who may quote brief
passages in a review.

First Large Print Edition

The Large Print Edition published
in accord with the standards of the N.A.V.H.

The characters and events in this book are fictitious. Any
similarity to real persons, living or dead, is coincidental
and not intended by the author.

Library of Congress Cataloging-in-Publication Data

Patterson, James.
    Sam's letters to Jennifer : a novel / by James
    Patterson. — 1st ed.
        p. cm.
    ISBN 0-316-71057-1 (hc) /
    ISBN 0-316-00074-4 (lg. print)
    I. Title.
PS3566.A822S26 2004
813'.54 — dc22   2003020701

10 9 8 7 6 5 4 3 2 1

Q-FF

Printed in the United States of America

Special thanks to Florence Kelleher, who found out *what little* she didn't already know about Lake Geneva, Wisconsin. And for Lynn Colomello. And most of all for Maxine Paetro, my friend and confidante, who helped to shape and *max*imize *Letters* from the beginning, almost to the end.

PROLOGUE
Just Like Always

SAM AND I are sitting on a mostly deserted beach on Lake Michigan a little north of the Drake Hotel in Chicago. The Drake is filled with treasured memories for both of us, and we had dinner at our favorite table there earlier. I need to be with Sam tonight, because it's one year since, well, everything happened that shouldn't have happened — it's one year since Danny died.

"This is the spot where I met Danny, Sam. In May, six years ago," I say.

Sam is a good listener who holds eye contact beautifully and is almost always interested in what I have to say, even when

3

I'm being a bore, like now. We've been best friends since I was two, maybe even before that. Just about everybody calls us "the cutest couple," which is a little too saccharine for both of our tastes. But it happens to be true.

"Sam, it was freezing that night Danny and I met, and I had a terrible cold. To make it worse, I had been locked out of our apartment by my old boyfriend Chris, that awful beast."

"That despicable brute, that creep," Sam contributes. "I never liked Chris. Can you tell?"

"So this nice guy, Danny, comes jogging by and he asks if I'm all right. I'm coughing and crying and a total mess. And I say, 'Do I look like I'm all right? Mind your own blanking business. You're not going to pick me up, if that's what you're thinking. Scram!'" I snorted a laugh Sam's way.

"That's where I got my nickname, 'Scram.' Anyway, Danny came back on the second

4

half of his run. He said he could hear me coughing for two miles down the beach. He brought me coffee, Sam. He ran up the beach with a hot cup of coffee for a complete stranger."

"Yes, but a beautiful stranger, you have to admit."

I stopped talking, and Sam hugged me and said, "You've been through so much. It's awful and it's unfair. I wish I could wave a magic wand and make it all better for you."

I pulled out a folded, wrinkled envelope from the pocket of my jeans. "Danny left this for me. In Hawaii. One year ago today."

"Go ahead, Jennifer. Let it out. I want to hear everything tonight."

I opened the letter and began to read. I was already starting to choke up.

Dear, wonderful, gorgeous Jennifer . . .
You're the writer, not me, but I had to try to put down some of my feelings

about your incredible news. I always thought that you couldn't possibly make me any happier, but I was wrong.

Jen, I'm flying so high right now I can't believe what I'm feeling. I am, without a doubt, the luckiest man in the world. I married the best woman, and now I'm going to have the best baby with her. How could I not be a pretty good dad, with all that going for me? I will be. I promise.

I love you even more today than I did yesterday, and you wouldn't believe how much I loved you yesterday.

I love you, and our little "peanut." . . .

Danny.

Tears started to roll down my cheeks. "I'm such a big baby," I said. "I'm pathetic."

"No, you're one of the strongest women I know. You've lost so much, and you're still fighting."

"Yeah, but I'm losing the battle. I'm losing. I'm losing real bad, Sam."

Then Sam pulled me close and hugged me, and for the moment at least, it was all better — just like always.

PART ONE
The Letters

One

~

MY TWO-BEDROOM apartment was in a prewar building in Wrigleyville. Danny and I had loved everything about it — the city views, proximity to the real Chicago, the way we'd furnished the place. I was spending more and more time there, "holed up," my good friends said. They also said I was "married to my job," "a basket case," "a hopeless workaholic," "the new spinster," and "romantically challenged" — to name just a few of their more memorable jibes. All of them, unfortunately, were true, and I could have added some others to the list.

I was trying not to think about what had happened, but it was hard. For several months after Danny's death I kept having this terrible, obsessive thought: *I can't breathe without you, Danny.*

Even after a year and a half I had to force myself not to think of the accident, and everything that happened after it.

I had finally begun to date — Teddy, a tall-drink-of-water editorial writer from the *Trib;* sportsaholic Mike, whom I met at a Cubs game; Corey, a blind date from the tenth circle of hell. I hated dating, but I needed to move on, right? I had a lot of good friends — couples, single women, a few guys who were just buddies. Really. Honest. I was doing okay, I told everybody, which was mostly crap, and my good friends knew it.

My best friends in the world, Kylie and Danny Borislow, were there for me again and again; I loved Kylie and Danny and I owe them so much.

So, anyhow, my deadline for that day's incredible, awe-inspiring column in the *Tribune* was three hours away and I was in a jam. I'd already tossed three ideas into the recycle bin and was staring at a blank screen again. The really tricky thing about writing a "witty" newspaper column is that between Mark Twain, Oscar Wilde, and Dorothy Parker, everything worth saying has already been said, and said better than I could ever say it.

So I pushed myself up from the sofa, put some Ella Fitzgerald on the Bose, and dialed up the air conditioner to high cool. I took a sip of coffee from my Uncommon Ground take-out cup. Found it sooo-ooo good. There is always hope in small things.

Then I paced around the living room in my writer's outfit du jour: one of Danny's Michigan U. jogging suits and my lucky red writing socks. I was dragging on a Newport Light, the latest in a string of bad habits I'd picked up lately. Mike Royko once said that you're only as good as your last column, and that's the truth that dogs me. That and my anorexic twenty-nine-year-old editor, Debbie, a former London tabloid reporter who wears Versace everything and Prada everything else with her Morgenthal Frederics glasses.

The point is, I really care about the column. I work hard to be original, make the words sing on occasion, and get the work in on time, without fail.

So I hadn't answered the phone that had been ringing on and off for hours. I *had* cursed at it a couple of times, though.

It's hard to be fresh three times a week, fifty weeks a year, but, of course, that's the job the *Trib* pays me to do. And in my case, the job is also pretty much my life.

Funny, then, how many readers write to say that my life is so glamorous, they'd like to swap places — wait, was that an idea?

The sudden crash behind my head was Sox, my year-old mostly tabby cat, knocking *The Devil in the White City* down from a bookshelf. That startled Euphoria, who'd been snoozing on the very typewriter F. Scott Fitzgerald supposedly wrote *Tender Is the Night* on. Or something like that. Maybe Zelda wrote *Save Me the Last Waltz* on it?

And when the phone rang again, I grabbed it.

When I realized who was on the line, a shock ran through me. I called up an old picture of John Farley, a family friend from Lake Geneva in Wisconsin. The minister's voice cracked when he said hello and I had the strange sensation that he was crying.

"It's Sam," he said.

Two

~

I GRIPPED the phone receiver tightly with both hands. "What's wrong?"

I heard him suck in a breath before he spoke again. "Ah, there's no good way to tell you this, Jennifer. Your grandmother has taken a fall," he told me. "It's not good."

"Oh, no!" I said, and sent my thoughts out to Lake Geneva, a resort community about an hour and a half north of Chicago. Lake Geneva was where I'd spent most of the summers of my childhood, some of the best times of my life.

"She was all alone in the house, so no one knows for sure what happened," he

16

continued. "Just that she's in a coma. Can you come up to the lake, Jennifer?"

The news was a jolt. I'd just spoken to Sam two days before. We'd joked about my love life and she'd threatened to send me a box of anatomically approximate gingerbread men. Sam is a comedian, always has been.

It took me all of five minutes to change my clothes and throw a few things into a duffel bag. It took me a little longer than that to catch and cage Euphoria and Sox for an unexpected journey.

Then I was gunning the old Jag up Addison Street, heading toward I-94 North. The '96 Jaguar Vanden Plas is a midnight blue sedan that was our pride and joy, Danny's and mine. It's a handsome thing with a quirky detail; the car has dual gas tanks.

I was trying to think about everything *but* Sam. My grandmother was the only one I had left now, the only family.

Sam was my best friend after my mother

died when I was twelve. Her own marriage to Grandpa Charles made me and everyone else want whatever it was that they had. My grandfather wasn't the easiest guy to get to know, but once you broke through to him, he was great. Danny and I had toasted and roasted them at their fiftieth-anniversary gala at the Drake. Two hundred friends stood to applaud when my seventy-one-year-old grandfather dipped Sam low and kissed her passionately on the dance floor.

When Grandpa Charles retired from his legal practice, he and Sam stayed at Lake Geneva more than in Chicago. After a while, they didn't get so many visitors. Even fewer came after my grandfather died four years ago and she moved to the lake full-time. When that happened, people said that Sam would die soon, too.

But she didn't. She'd been doing fine — until now.

At about 8:15 I got on Route 50 West and took it to 12, a local two-laner that skirts

Lake Geneva — the BPOE, "best place on earth." After three miles, I turned off 12 onto Route NN. Lakeland Medical Center was just a couple of minutes away and I tried to prepare myself.

"We're close, Sam," I whispered.

Three

~

REALLY BAD THINGS happen in threes, I was thinking as I arrived at the Lakeland Medical Center. Then I tried to banish the thought from my mind. *Don't go there, Jennifer.*

I got out of the car and started uphill to the main entrance. I remembered that many years before, I had been there to have a fishing hook removed from just above my eyebrow. I was seven at the time, and it was Sam who brought me.

Once I was inside, I tried to get my bearings, taking in the horseshoe-shaped ICU with patients' rooms on three sides. The head nurse, a thin, fortyish woman with pink-framed glasses, pointed out my grand-mother's room. "We're so glad you're here," she said. "I enjoy your column, by the way. We all do."

"Thank you," I said, and smiled. "You're very kind. That's nice to hear."

I walked quickly down the corridor to Sam's room. I slid the door open and entered. "Oh, Sam," I whispered the second I saw her. "What happened to you?"

It was so awful to see the tubes in her arms and the banks of beeping medical equipment. But at least Sam was alive. Though she looked diminished and gray, and as fragile as a dream.

"It's Jennifer," I whispered. "I'm here now. I'm right here." I took her hand in mine. "I know you can hear me. I'll do the talking for now. I'm going to keep talking until you open your eyes."

After a few minutes, I heard the door slide open behind me. I turned to see the Reverend John Farley. His thick white hair was askew, his smile tremulous. He was still a handsome man, though stooped now. "Hello, Jennifer," he whispered, and welcomed me with a warm hug.

We walked out into the hallway and suddenly I was remembering how close he had been to my grandparents.

"It's so good to see you. What have you heard about Sam?" I asked.

He shook his head. "Well, she hasn't opened her eyes, and that's not a good sign, Jennifer. I'm sure Dr. Weisberg will have more to tell you tomorrow. I've been here most of the day, ever since I heard."

Then he handed me a key. "This is for you. Your grandmother's house."

He hugged me again, whispering that he had to get some sleep before he wound up there as a patient. Then he left and I slipped back into Sam's room. I still couldn't believe this had happened.

She had always been so strong, almost never sick, always the one who took care of everybody else — especially me. I sat for a long while just listening to her breathe, looking at her beautiful face, remembering all the times I'd come to Lake Geneva. Sam had always reminded me a little of Katharine Hepburn, and we'd seen all her movies together, though she vehemently denied there was any resemblance.

I felt so scared. How could I lose Sam now? It seemed as if I had just lost Danny. Tears began to stream down my cheeks again. "Shit," I whispered under my breath.

I waited until I got back some control and then I moved close to her. I kissed both of her cheeks and stared at her face. I kept expecting Sam's eyes to open, for her to speak. But she didn't. Oh, why was this happening?

"I'm going back to the house. Pancakes for breakfast," I whispered. "I'll see you in the morning. You hear me? I'll *see* you in the morning. First thing, bright and early."

One of my tears fell onto Sam's cheek, but it just trickled down her face.

"Good night, Sam," I said.

Four

~

I HAVE LITTLE or no memory of the drive from Lakeland Medical to Knollwood Road on Lake Geneva. I was just suddenly *there* at my grandmother's house, and it felt incredibly familiar and safe.

A century of parked cars had worn away the grass under an ancient oak in the side yard, and that's where I brought the Jag to a stop. I shut off the ignition and just sat for a minute or two, hoping to gather myself before I went inside.

To my left, the lawn flowed downhill to the shoreline. I could see the long white dock jutting out onto the moonlit and

24

glassy surface of Lake Geneva. The water was a mirror for the star-pricked sky.

To my right was the old white clapboard lake house, porches all around, rising up to two asymmetrical stories of added-on dormered rooms. My grandparents' home sweet home. I knew every curve and angle of the house and the view from every porch and window.

I released my seat belt and stepped out of the car into the humid summer air. And that was when the fragrance of the casa blanca lilies hit me. They were Sam's and my favorites — the prize of the garden, where we had spent many a night sitting on the stone bench, smelling the flowers, gazing up at the sky.

It was here that she'd tell me stories about Lake Geneva — how it freezes east to west, how when they were digging ground for the golf course at Geneva National they unearthed a cemetery.

Sam had stories about everything, and no one told them the way she could. *This* was where I became a writer. Right here at this house, and Sam was my inspiration.

I was suddenly overwhelmed. Tears I'd been holding in broke free. I dropped down to my knees on the hardpan parking area. I whispered Sam's name. I had the terrible thought that she might not ever come back to this house. I couldn't stand it.

I had always thought of myself as strong — and now this. Somebody was trying to break me. Well, it wasn't going to happen.

I don't know how long I stayed there in the parking area. Eventually I stood, opened the trunk, shouldered my duffel bag, and started inside with the cats. They were vocalizing from their cages and I was about to liberate them when I saw a light go on in a house a hundred yards or so down the shoreline. A second later the light winked out.

I got the feeling that somebody was watching me. But who knew I was there?

Not even Sam.

Five

~

SAM'S HOUSE was my favorite place in the world, the sanest, and always the safest — until tonight anyway.

Now everything seemed off-kilter. The kitchen was dark, so I threw on the light switch. Then I put down the cats and opened their cage doors.

The girls sprang forward like little race-horses out of the gate. Sox is three-quarters alley cat, one-quarter loudmouth Siamese. Euphoria is an all-white longhair with green eyes and a smoochy nature. My hands were still shaking from stress as I fed the two of them.

Then I walked from room to room, and it all looked exactly the same.

An old burnished hardwood floor secured with square-headed nails. A chaotic mass of houseplants crowding the bay window in the dining room. An astonishing view of the lake. Books spread everywhere. *Bel Canto*. Queen Noor's memoir. *A Short History of Nearly Everything*.

And the artifacts that Sam and I loved: antique ice tongs from the days when blocks of ice were shipped by horse teams to Milwaukee and Chicago; old snowshoes; paintings of the round pink crab apple trees along the lake and of the old train depot.

I heaved a big sigh. This really was home to me, more than anywhere else, especially now that Danny was gone from our apartment in Chicago.

I took my duffel bag upstairs to "my room," with its views down onto the lake.

I was about to drop the bag on the vanity table when I saw that it was already occupied.

What is this?

There were a dozen banded packets of envelopes, probably a hundred envelopes in all, maybe more. Each was numbered and addressed to me.

My heart started thudding as I guessed about the letters. For years, I had been asking Sam to tell me her story. I wanted to hear it, and record it for my own children to hear. And now here it was. Had she known what was going to happen to her? Had she been feeling sick?

I didn't bother to undress. I just slid into the soft folds of bedcovers and took a stack of the letters into my lap.

I stared at my name written in blue-inked script. Sam's familiar handwriting. Then I turned over the first envelope and carefully peeled open the flap.

The letter inside was written on beautiful white linen paper.

I took a deep breath, and noticed I was trembling as I began to read.

Six

~

Dear Jennifer,
You've just left after our most recent "girls" weekend together and my heart is full of you. Actually, I decided to write this when we were saying good-bye at the car. It just came to me.

I was looking into your eyes and I was struck by a feeling so hard that it physically hurt. I thought about how close we are, always have been, and how it would be a shame, almost a betrayal of our friendship, if I didn't tell you some things about my life.

So I've made a decision, Jen, to tell you secrets that I've never told anyone before.

Some are good; a few you might find, well, I guess *shocking* is the word I'm looking for.

I'm in your room right now, looking out at our lake, drinking a mug of that heady spearmint tea we both like, and it makes me happy to think of you reading my letters a few at a time, just the way I'm writing them. I can see your face as I write this, Jennifer. I can see your lovely smile.

Right now, I'm thinking about love: the hot, crazy kind that turns your chest into a bell and your heart into a clapper. But also the more enduring kind that comes from knowing someone else deeply and letting yourself be known. What you had with Danny.

I guess I believe in both kinds of love, both kinds at the same time and with the same person.

By now you're probably wondering why I'm going on about love. You're twirling your hair around your finger, aren't you?

Aren't you, Jennifer?

I want, I *need,* to talk to you about your grandfather and me, sweetheart. So here goes.

The truth is, I never really loved Charles.

Seven

Jennifer,

Now that I've written that difficult sentence, and you had to read it . . .

Please take a good look at the old black-and-white photo I've clipped to this letter. It was taken the day the direction of my life changed forever.

I remember it was a humid morning in July. I know it was humid because my hair had sprung into those stupid Shirley Temple curls that I just hated at the time. See the apothecary jars inside the plate-glass window behind me? I'm standing in front of Dad's pharmacy, squinting in the sun. My dress is blue and a little faded. Note my hands-on-hips stance and the self-possessed grin. That's who I was. Confident. A little forward. Naive. Full of potential to be anything I wanted to be. Or so I believed.

Here's what I was thinking at that very moment.

My mother had died some years before and I was managing the store that summer. But the next year I was going to leave Lake Geneva, go to the University of Chicago, and eventually become a doctor. That's right, I planned to be an obstetrician. And I was proud of myself for working hard to make it come true.

After this picture was taken, I followed my father back into the dimly lit and narrow store. I swept the wooden floor with Dust Down compound and set the daily newspapers out on the radiator near the door.

I was sponging down the marble counter at the soda fountain when the door opened and slammed shut with a sharp bang.

It would be accurate to say that my whole life changed right there, with that bang!

I looked up, scowling, and my eyes locked with those of a most handsome young man. I noticed everything about him in a flash: that he was limping, and I wondered why; that he was dressed in expensive clothes, which probably meant he was a lakeshore person, a summer visitor; that he looked at me hard — *bang* — like a shot to the heart.

We continued to make twenty-twenty eye contact as he slowly walked to the soda fountain, then sat down on one of the swivel stools. On closer look, he wasn't conventionally handsome. His nose was a little too wide and his ears stuck out some. But he had jet-black hair and dark blue eyes and a nice mouth. That's exactly what I thought. I remember it to this day.

I took his lunch order. Then I forced myself to turn my back and I made him an egg salad sandwich, no onions, extra mayo on the side.

I put coffee on to perk, feeling his eyes on me. I could almost feel steam coming off the back of my neck.

I had lots of things to do that morning. Cartons of Listerine, Ipana, Burma-Shave all needed unpacking, and my father had asked me to help him measure out prescriptions.

But I was stuck there at the soda fountain because that boy wouldn't leave. And to be completely honest, I didn't want him to.

He finally pushed back his plate and asked for another "cuppa joe," which made me laugh.

"You're beautiful, you know that?" he said as I poured more coffee into his cup. "I think we've met. Maybe in a dream I had? Or maybe I just want to know you so badly that I'll say anything right now."

"I'm Samantha," I managed to say. "We've never met."

He gave me a brilliant smile. "Hi, Samantha. I'm Charles," he said, and extended a hand for me to shake. "Will you do a soldier a big favor? Have dinner with me tonight."

Who could say no to that?

Eight

~

Jen,

Charles and I had dinner that night at the posh and wonderful Lake Geneva Inn, where you and I still have two- and three-hour lunches. I'd never been inside the place before and I was dazzled by the grandeur, the lights, the *class*. (Remember, I was all of eighteen.) Candles winked, glasses clinked, silent waiters served lavish dishes, and the wine kept coming — champagne, too.

Charles seemed so much older than his twenty-one years, and I was fascinated by everything he said and everything he *didn't* say that night. After much urging

by me, he finally told me about the bullet
he'd taken in Sicily, and he hinted at a
deeper hurt that he said he'd tell me about
someday.

I found this promise of future intimacy
by Charles irresistible.

At eighteen, I was very impressionable.
I was a small-town girl, and being with
Charles opened me to a much larger
world, one that intrigued me. How could
it not?

You have to understand that life felt
very precious during the war, Jen. Gail
Snyder's brother had been killed at Pearl
Harbor, my uncle Harmon had been
wounded, and nearly every boy I knew
was fighting overseas. (I say "boy" because
that's what most of them were, and that's
what war has always meant to me — a
place where boys are sent to die.) It
seemed a miracle that Charles had come
home and that we had met that summer.

We went out every night for a month
and a half, and he usually stopped by for

lunch as well. I got my spunk back and began to have more fun than I'd ever had before. Charles talked easily about all the countries in Europe he'd seen and cracked me up by singing popular American songs with a French accent. He was moody occasionally, but it mostly seemed a dream come true. He was so handsome and quick-witted, and a war hero.

Then one moonlit night on the lake, Charles whispered that he loved me and always would: he was so certain of it that he convinced me. When he proposed marriage nine weeks after our first date, I almost bounded over the moon. I shrieked, and he took that to mean yes. Then Charles kissed me tenderly and slid a large emerald-cut diamond on my ring finger. Oh, I was the happiest girl in the world.

We were married on a late September day, the sun shining brightly one moment, disappearing behind woolly gray clouds the next. The changing light was like a

curtain falling between acts of a play,
and the wedding, too, felt like a dazzling
Broadway production. I was mad for
Charles. Nothing felt completely real, but
it was wonderful.

The ceremony was held at the Lake
Geneva Country Club. We weren't mem-
bers and my dad couldn't pay for a wedding like that, but the Stanfords could and
did, so we deferred most decisions to my
in-laws-to-be.

But my dad *had* interceded with Mrs.
Sine in town, who made the most beautiful white silk dress. It was high-necked
with dozens of buttons down the back
and more buttons from the sleeves to the
wrists, and a long, full skirt that bunched
around my feet.

You know it well, Jen, because you wore
it when you married Danny.

I can still see it. The country club, all
our guests, Charles with his slicked-back
jet-black hair, his ramrod-straight posture.
My dad handed me off to the handsome

groom. An Illinois Supreme Court judge officiated. I shyly whispered my wedding vows, meaning them with all my heart.

Charles and I exchanged rings, and then he lifted my veil to kiss me. There were cheers and applause, and everyone spilled out of the main country club building and onto the sprawling lawn. Billowy white tents had been set up near the edge of the lake. The best catered food money could buy was served and a top band from Chicago played Benny Goodman and Glenn Miller.

Half the guests had polished manners and wore clothes that had been designed in Chicago and New York; my friends and family wore their Sunday best and stared down at their shoes a little too often. But the champagne worked its magic. We danced and danced on the lawn, and huge flocks of migrating geese winged across the sky. My friends fluttered around me as the sun set and they told me that I was the envy of them all. I understood what they meant, and I had to agree.

It was just perfect, Jennifer.

Or so I believed for that one glorious night, my wedding night on our beautiful Lake Geneva.

Nine

~

I READ only a couple of the letters, as I'd been told. Then I fell asleep in my clothes, no doubt dreaming of Sam, past and present. I awoke with the vaguest feeling of dread, as if I'd been shaken out of an awful nightmare, a fantasy not of my choosing.

It took a moment to place the apple green walls and the fluffy mohair throw over my legs, but then I got it. I was at Sam's house. I was supposed to be safe and protected here, happy too. I always had been in the past.

There was a weight on my chest — Sox in deep slumber.

I had just dislodged the cat when a high-pitched, almost bloodcurdling scream came through the thin panes of the bedroom window. Was someone being murdered outside? Of course not — but what was that awful noise?

I bounded over to the window, parted the curtain, and peered out into the front yard. It was early morning.

I couldn't see too much out the window, mostly shadows and wisps of mist coming off the lake. A row of shingled houses stretched south. Then I saw and heard a man yelling with the exuberance of a ten-year-old. He charged across the lawn of a house maybe a hundred yards down the shoreline.

The running man cleared the lawn quickly and nimbly, negotiated the length of rickety-looking dock painted white, and, without breaking stride, performed a shallow dive into the lake.

What a neat dive it was. And what an odd scene for so early in the morning.

I watched for a minute or so as he

stroked a smooth freestyle before disappearing into the mist. He was a good swimmer — graceful, strong. That made me think of Danny. He'd been a great swimmer, too.

I turned away. I was awake now, so I pulled off the day before's clothes and tugged on clean jeans and a blue Cubs sweatshirt from the top of my duffel bag. I picked up Sam's letters, which had fallen to the floor. I remembered "I never really loved Charles." I couldn't deal with that one yet. I had loved my grandfather. How was it possible that Sam hadn't?

I went downstairs to the homey, golden oak kitchen where so many summer mornings had started. I fixed coffee and called the hospital to check on Sam, and to make sure her doctor could see me later that morning. Sam was holding stable. She still hadn't opened her eyes, though.

I slammed around the familiar kitchen, making breakfast for myself: Grape-Nuts, orange juice, a "cuppa joe," whole wheat toast with sweet butter. I fed the cats — and peeked to see if the swimmer had returned. He hadn't. Maybe I'd made him up.

While I sipped the last of my coffee, I watched Lake Geneva. God, it was beautiful. The early fog had lifted some. *And what is this?* The swimmer was hoisting himself up on his dock and was sluicing water off his body with the edge of his hands. I noticed something I hadn't seen before. He was naked.

Well, he had a decent body, whoever he was. Obviously, *he* liked it, too. Typical male narcissism, not to mention thoughtlessness. "Jerk," I mumbled.

Maybe ten minutes later, the Jag was purring softly under the oak. I set a big bunch of freshly picked flowers next to me on the passenger seat. I hit the road to see Sam. She had some questions to answer.

Ten

~

I SHAVED a couple of minutes off the usual fifteen-minute run to the hospital. Once I was there, I found my way to the ICU. Visitors were already gathering at the nurses' station, but I caught the attention of one of the physicians. Dr. Mark Ormson apologized but told me that I should wait. Sam's doctor was examining her right now.

There was a coffee machine in the waiting room around the corner. I pressed quarters into it and was thinking that I needed to see Sam but that I *didn't* need any more coffee.

Out of the corner of my eye, I saw a man of about seventy-five, tanned, with a well-trimmed beard. He waved, then rose from one of the linked plastic chairs and walked toward me. It was Shep Martin, Sam's lawyer and a neighbor on the lake.

We sat down, and when he started talking about Sam, it was obvious that Shep was as surprised and shook up about her condition as everybody else seemed to be.

"I've adored Sam for forty years," he told me. "You know, I met her right here at the hospital." Shep then told me a story that sent shivers racing up and down my back and neck.

"One night, this was about forty years ago, Jennifer, I was out of town when I learned that my father had been in a car crash. I got to the hospital the next morning — only to find a woman I'd never met before sitting beside my critically injured father. The woman was holding his hand. I didn't know what to say.

"Fortunately, Sam spoke first. She explained that she had been visiting a friend the previous night. Your grandfather was out of town. She was passing my father's room when a nurse came out. The nurse mistook Sam for my sister, Adele. She gripped her by the wrist and brought her to my father's bedside, saying, 'Your father is asking for you.'

"My dad was semiconscious or worse. He never realized that Sam was a stranger, and she never set him straight. Sam stayed the entire night with my father — just because he needed someone."

As Shep finished his story, I heard someone call my name, and it startled me some.

I turned and saw a doctor standing in the entrance to the waiting room. It was Max Weisberg, blond and clean-shaven, wearing green scrubs and holding a chart in front of him. Max is a few years older than I am, but I've known him since we were kids on the lake.

His expression was distressingly grave as he walked toward me and extended his hand. "Jennifer, I'm glad you're here," he said. "You can go in and see your grandmother now."

Eleven

~

ON THE WAY to Sam's room, Max Weisberg answered most of my pressing questions, but then he told me to go inside with her. I still had the freshly cut flowers in my arms as I walked up close to Sam's bed and bent down low so that maybe she could smell them.

"Hi, it's Jennifer. I'm here to pester you again. I'm going to keep coming until you *tell* me not to," I began.

"*Everybody* in town is asking about you. They want you to get well immediately, if not sooner. We really miss you, Sam. I'm speaking for the whole town, by the way. . . . But more than anybody else, I miss you."

I found a nice place for the flowers on the windowsill near the bed. "I got your letters," I said. "How could I miss them?" I reached over and touched Sam's cheek, then kissed it.

"Thank you — for sharing the letters with me. I promise I won't read them in one gulp, though I want to."

I stared at Sam's face. I thought I knew everything about her, but obviously I didn't. She was still so pretty — real down-to-earth beauty. My eyes started to tear again, and I felt a pain in the center of my chest. I couldn't speak for a moment. I loved her so much. She and Danny were my best friends, the only ones I ever really let inside. And now this had to happen.

"Let me tell *you* a story," I finally said. "This goes back to when I was four or five. We would drive over to the lake from Madison half a dozen times every summer.

Those times at the lake *were* the summer for me.

"Do you remember, Sam? When we used to leave, every single visit, you would stand on the porch and call out, 'Bye, I love you guys.'

"And I would lean out the car window and call back, 'Bye, Grandma, I love you, too! Bye, Grandma, I love you!' What you didn't know is that I would keep repeating it all the way home — 'Bye, Grandma, I love you. Bye, I love you.' I *do* love you, Sam. Do you hear me? I love you so much. And I refuse to say *bye*."

Twelve

~

I HATED to leave Sam but I'd made a lunch date that I wanted to keep. I drove out of the hospital parking lot and was soon cruising down the main street in town.

Lake Geneva is like a toy village, only life-size, and I've seldom met anyone, except the worst cynic, who didn't love it. The wide and busy street is lined with pretty good restaurants and nice shops selling antiques, and the shining lake glitters magnificently as a backdrop.

I stopped at the light and watched people drift in laughing clumps along the sidewalk, overlapping my memories of recent summers I'd spent doing the same with Danny. *Oh, Danny, Danny, I wish you were here.*

I parked in front of what used to be my great-granddad's pharmacy and entered the cool interior. John Farley was waiting for me at a booth with red leather seats in the back of the store. He looked dashing with his thick white hair, and was wearing a striped blue and yellow rugby shirt and khakis.

He rose when he saw me. "You look like hell," he said, beaming.

"That means a lot, coming from an expert on hell," I said, smiling for the first time all day. While many clergy seem to have gotten life's lessons from books, John was as in touch with reality as a good Chicago shrink. We ordered grilled cheese sandwiches and chocolate shakes from a teenage girl who had no idea I was seeing the fountain through an old sepia-colored filter, remembering Sam's description of meeting my grandfather there.

"What kind of man was my grandfather?" I asked John after our lunch arrived.

"He was a fine lawyer, crooked golfer, good family man. He was what you would call a man's man," he said.

"Charles and Sam met right here," I said. "Not ten feet from where we're sitting."

John must have seen something sad cross my face. He reached out and took my hands in his. "When I think about your grandfather, what jumps out at me is that he couldn't stand to get his clothes dirty, Jennifer, but he was always out in the yard raking or moving rocks around for your grandma. Or stacking firewood or tinkering with her car.

"Meanwhile, she took care of him. Cooked what he liked to eat. Kept his spirits up. In their own way, they were devoted to each other."

I nodded, and wondered if he was telling me the whole story. "And what about Sam? What kind of woman was she?"

John Farley had the most dazzling smile. "Your grandmother is the strongest person I know. I'm sure she's going to get through this, Jennifer. Don't ever count Sam out."

Thirteen

~

THAT AFTERNOON I was back at Sam's house, and I was trying not to let what had happened get me down. I was thinking about making one of Sam's famous "wacky cakes" and then eating it all by myself. The huge oak tree out front cast a soft shade over the front yard. Just like always. A couple strolled along the footpath that encircled the lake; sailboats blew across the water, pulled by their colorful sails.

A rosy-cheeked older man sat out in a wheelchair at the water's edge, tossing a green tennis ball for a brown terrier mutt. The dog brought the ball back every single time. The man finally saw me, and as people on the lake do, he waved.

I waved back, then went inside. I returned to the front porch with a big glass of lemonade and a packet of Sam's letters.

I had so many questions about Sam and my grandfather now. *I never really loved Charles.* Was that true? Was it possible? What other secrets did the letters hold?

I settled into a wicker rocker, untied the packet, and gave the string to Sox, who took it off into the bushes to kill.

Then, with a breeze riffling my hair, I began to read the story of who my grandmother really was.

The first few letters were notes about Sam's garden, her feelings about a provocative column I wrote on the post office disaster in Chicago, some thoughts on President Clinton, whom Sam both adored and was terribly disappointed in.

Then I picked up the thread of her life story — and Sam dropped another bombshell on my head. Geez, I had hardly recovered from the last one.

Fourteen

Jennifer,

This could be the worst of the letters that I'll write.

Charles and I honeymooned in Miami, as you know. We stayed at the Fountainebleau, a wonderful old hotel on Collins Avenue, right on the beach. But Charles was unhappy the whole time we were there. He complained that the hotel staff was too servile, the food too rich, the sand too sandy. To put it mildly, he found fault with everything.

And he especially found fault with me.

On our third night there, right after dinner, we were on the small terrace outside our room, listening to the ocean pound against the jetties. Charles had had several drinks.

I was trying to make conversation. "I enjoyed meeting that couple from North Carolina. We had some good laughs, didn't we?"

His face darkened with a storm that seemed to come out of nowhere. He looked me straight in the eye. "If you ever stand up against me, if you ever cross me in any way, if you ever become a bore or a simpleton, I will leave you and without a dime." Then he raised his right hand and slapped me across the face. Quite hard. Bone-jarring. I think it was the first time I had ever been hit in my life.

Then Charles thundered inside, leaving me devastated on the terrace. I sat outside for a long time, listening to the surf of the Atlantic Ocean, or maybe it was the blood pounding in my ears. I wanted to throw up, to run home, but how could I?

Jennifer, I was crushed and terribly confused. Do you understand? I'd left my home, all my friends, so that I could be with Charles. Things were very different back then, especially for small-town girls. A woman didn't get divorced, not even if she was struck.

I grew up that first night of our honeymoon; I saw our future together and felt there was little I could do to change it. But I did do one thing. Before we left Miami, I told Charles that if he ever hit me again, I would leave him on the spot and damn the consequences. Everybody would know what a bastard and bully he was.

After the honeymoon, Charles and I moved to a large apartment in Chicago. It still wasn't very good between us, though. Once he'd passed the bar, your grandfather joined the family firm. Soon I gave birth to your mother, then to your aunt Val. But, Jennifer, I lived for the summers, when I always returned to Lake Geneva.

But I dreaded the weekends, when Charles would come up from Chicago. He brought his moods with him, though he rarely raised his hand to me. He was selfish and enjoyed putting me down in front of the children and friends of ours. But he did provide for us, and he eventually did make good on the promise he'd made to tell me the dark secret in his past. What Charles would never tell me were the secrets in his present, the girlfriends he had in Chicago and elsewhere.

I'm sorry to have to tell you this, but you wanted to hear my story.

Fifteen

~

Sweetheart,

Let me tell you some other things about your grandfather so you can understand how he came to be the man that he was. The husband, even the grandfather.

Picture Charles telling me about what he called "sins of the father," events that shaped his life — and mine. It was three years after we were married. Your mother was in her crib in the next room, and she was such a good little sleeper. Charles and I were in bed, and cars whooshed by in the rain, lighting our faces with headlights as they passed our window in the Chicago apartment.

It was on this dreary night that Charles finally told me about the transforming event of his life. It had happened when he was just sixteen, and it is an incredible story.

Charles's parents had thrown a party in their imposing home for their older son, Peter, who had just graduated from prep school. It was after dinner and the guests had moved to the library for coffee. Peter was opening his gifts and Charles made a careless remark to his father that his older brother always seemed to get the best of everything.

Arthur Stanford just snapped. He turned on Charles, called him an ingrate. He then said that it was time for Charles to know the truth. "You're not even our son. You're adopted!" his father yelled at him. Just like that, in front of everyone in the family. The party stopped, and in the brittle silence that followed, Charles ran upstairs to his room. His father was right behind him. When they reached the top landing,

Charles screamed, "It isn't true! I know it isn't true!"

Arthur Stanford had calmed some by now. "Believe me, Charles, I'm not your father. I'm your *uncle*," he said. "Your father is my brother Ben. He got a girl pregnant, a little nobody from nowhere."

"You're l-l-lying," Charles stammered pitifully.

"Go and ask your father then," Arthur said. "It's time you knew him anyway. The last I heard, he was working at the Murray Tap. It's a gin mill in Milwaukee." Then Arthur Stanford lowered his voice. "Caroline and I took you in. We've tried to love you, Charlie. We do our best."

That night, when he was just sixteen, Charles went to the Wabash and Adams Street train station. He bought a dollar ticket and caught the North Shore Line to Milwaukee.

Inside our bedroom, Jennifer, passing headlights lit Charles's face and I could see his eyes lit up in terrible pain. My heart went out to him. If I couldn't completely forgive him for everything, at least I understood what had happened to make him so angry, and occasionally cruel.

Charles continued his story, and some of the words were so vivid that I can remember them to this day.

He told me that the train ride ended two hours later. His uncle's phrase "a little nobody from nowhere" kept playing like a bad song in his head. He walked out onto Michigan Street at midnight. Two huge Milwaukee breweries were nearby, and the smothering smell of beer lay heavy in the air.

He asked directions, then walked east, until he found Murray Avenue. He almost passed the place he was looking for.

There was no sign out front, only a dirty window to the left of the door lit by a Miller High Life sign. Charles pulled on the creaking door and entered a barroom that was darker than the night outside. There was a long bar and a thick layer of smoke hovering over it.

Men who worked at the breweries and smelled like stale malt looked up at him. No one said anything or seemed to care that he was there.

When his eyes adjusted to the gloom, Charles climbed onto a covered stool. He sat in the shadows, taking in every detail: the dice cups on the bar — a few working men gambling for drinks — a sign that said

HOUSE SPECIALTY, PANTHER PISS.

Mostly he looked at the bartender, a rough-looking man with a scarred face but unmistakable Stanford features: the aristo-cratic, slightly crooked nose, the stuck-out ears. Charles told me, "The love I felt for him was almost painful."

As he watched, he saw his father short-change a customer and tell vulgar jokes about women, which made Charles's face go red.

Finally his father wiped down the bar with a greasy rag, leaned into Charles's face, and sneered. "Get the hell out of here, kid. Take a hike before I kick your ass across the river."

Charles opened his mouth, but nothing came out. The terrifying moment dragged on. His face burned, but Charles couldn't speak.

"A pansy," his father said to loud laughter. "Kid's a pansy. Now get the hell out of here!"

Shaking with emotion, Charles slid off the stool and left the bar. He never introduced himself to his father, never said a word. Not then, not ever.

I asked Charles, "How could you leave without talking to your father?" His voice got very flat, as if it hurt him to answer. He said that when he looked into his father's face, he saw Arthur's eyes — the same cold lack of feeling. And he knew that his own father had never loved him, and never would.

"I found him so easily," Charles said. "Why hadn't he ever found me?"

That night I took your grandfather in my arms, Jennifer. I understood that I was his only friend, whatever that meant to him. But as I pressed his head to my chest and smoothed his hair, I knew something else. I knew why Charles had married me. I was a little nobody from nowhere. Our marriage had been an act of defiance, Charles's way of putting his thumb in the Stanford family eye.

I was twenty-two years old, but I felt that my life was over.

Sixteen

~

I WAS REELING from Sam's sad story about my grandfather. As much as I had adored him, something about it rang true. Though she'd asked me to read the letters slowly, I wanted to know more. How could she have stayed with Charles all those years?

I was sitting in the kitchen and had just opened the flap of the next envelope when I was startled by a movement out of the corner of my eye and the sound of footfalls on the grass outside.

A man rounded the side of the house. The odd thing was, I thought I knew him but I didn't know from where. I went out onto the porch to see what he wanted.

His hair was light brown, with a soft tousled wave and a fiercely independent lock that sprang forward. He had very blue eyes.

"Hi," he said.

"Hi." Tentatively.

He was probably close to forty, wearing khaki shorts, a Notre Dame T-shirt, and the strangest old-man sandals.

Then it clicked. The last time I'd seen him, he wasn't wearing any clothes. This was the war-whooping swimmer.

"Jennifer?" he asked, and that threw me some. I was wondering how he knew my name when he put his hand on the banister and began to board Sam's front porch.

"Whoa," I said. "Do I know you?"

"Hey, I'm sorry. I'm Brendan Keller. I'm staying with my uncle Shep, four houses down. He said he ran into you at the hospital. *Brendan Keller?* You don't remember me, do you?"

I shook my head no. Then I nodded yes. It was all coming back. Brendan Keller and my cousin Eric had been a big part of my early summers at Lake Geneva. They were the brothers I never had. I'd followed them everywhere for a summer or two. They'd called me Scout, after the little girl in *To Kill a Mockingbird.*

I didn't remember having seen Brendan Keller since I was a little girl, though. I put out a hand. "Hey, long time."

The two of us wound up sitting on Sam's porch, talking over a couple of iced teas. Mostly we reminisced about Lake Geneva "back in the day." He knew my newspaper column, and I managed to get out of him that he was a doctor now.

"Eric and I called you Scout. You were very advanced for a ten-year-old. I think you'd actually read *To Kill a Mockingbird.*"

I laughed and cast my eyes down, embarrassed by something I couldn't quite get a handle on. He followed my gaze. "You're looking at my shoes."

"No, I —"

A slow smile spread across his face.

"I borrowed them from my uncle. Listen, speaking of Shep. He says the Lions Club is having a lobster boil over in Fontana. You're invited if you'd like."

I shook my head, almost a reflex. "No. I'm sorry. Tonight's not good. I'm writing my column. I'm way behind."

"If I change my shoes? I have really nice loafers. Sneakers? I could go barefoot."

I smiled. "I can't," I said. "Sorry. I have a deadline. Honestly."

Brendan stood up and set down his tea. "Okay. Well, I'm just down the road. I hope I'll see you around. *Brendan Keller.*"

"Scout." I smiled.

We mumbled good-byes and I waved as he walked back in the direction of his uncle's house. My former contemplative mood was blown. I put Sam's letters aside and went into the house.

I did some work that afternoon, and once or twice I thought about the lobster boil going on in Fontana without me. Eventually I made a salad for dinner, wondering why I'd been so hell-bent on eating alone.

But I knew why. Danny.

And our little "peanut."

Seventeen

~

THAT NIGHT I had the dream about Danny again, the one I hate more than anything, the dream where I am Danny but I'm also myself watching him.

It's always the same.

Danny is surfing on the north shore of Oahu, at one of the most beautiful beaches anywhere. The waves there are some of the biggest in the world one day, and then the ocean can be as flat as glass the next.

The bad part is that Danny is alone this day. He's supposed to be on vacation with me, but at the last minute I have to stay in Chicago to work on a big story for the *Tribune*. It's my choice to stay behind.

So there he is, waiting for his wave. And then he's up. The trouble is, the wave crests a lot faster than he expects. Suddenly he's slammed down on the seafloor some twenty feet below. Danny can't tell which way is up, which is down. He remembers a basic rule: one hand up, one hand down; feel for the bottom, feel for the air.

Then he's smashed to the ocean floor again, and he can't believe the strength of the wave. His ears are pounding and water's being rammed up his nose. His body is wrenched and twisted. His legs feel numb. Has he broken something? There's a terrible burning sensation in his lungs.

Then Danny lets go of everything . . . except for me and the baby. . . . He calls out: *Jennifer! Jennifer, help me! . . . Please help me, Jennifer!*

I woke up from the dream in my old room in Sam's house. I was in a cold sweat and my heart was racing. How could I put the past behind me when Danny was always in my dreams? I was late meeting him in Hawaii — everything that happened was my fault. Everything.

Eighteen

~

I LAY IN BED for a few minutes until I heard someone yelling outside. I finally perked myself up and parted the curtains of my bedroom window.

There he was, but at least he was wearing a bathing suit this morning. I watched him do a perfect racing dive from the dock into the lake. "Grow up," I muttered, then wondered when I had become such a grump.

I showered, dressed in yesterday's jeans and a *Tribune* softball T-shirt, clipped my hair into an upside-down ponytail. I walked outside into the fragrant summer morning. I needed to be outside and away from my nightmares.

There are about twelve hundred identical white docks around the twenty-six-mile circumference of Lake Geneva. Each dock is eight feet wide, thirty or so feet long, and nearly every house on the shore seems to have one. In November the docks are taken out of the lake for the winter; then come spring, they're painted and placed back in the water.

I took my coffee mug down to the end of Sam's dock, where I could watch the mallards and the swooping seagulls fishing for breakfast. Wisconsin is crazy for fish, mostly perch, some cod, and trout. This is the birthplace of the Republican party, but also the fiscally responsible Democrat William Proxmire, he of the Golden Fleece award given to government agencies that waste taxpayers' money. Interesting state.

Out on the lake, I could see Brendan Keller doing that strong freestyle I'd noticed the morning before. As I watched, he started swimming toward me. He got bigger in frame, closer, then he came right up

81

to the edge of Sam's dock and hauled himself up.

He shook himself off like a dog.

"*Hey!*" I said.

"You ought to get into a bathing suit and come for a swim, Scout. The water is unbelievable. That is not an exaggeration."

"Can't," I said, sounding a little like a poop even to myself. "Previous engagements."

"Working?" He smiled as he sluiced water off his body with the edges of his hands, as I'd seen him do before.

"I'm on my way to see Sam," I said. "I was just thinking about doing a column on government waste. Life of the mind, y'know."

"You eaten?"

"Drinking my breakfast this morning," I said, lifting my mug.

"You can do better than that," he said. "Now, don't give me any trouble. I make five-star blueberry pancakes. Really fast. Trust me, okay?"

Trust him? I opened and closed my mouth, but I was tired of sputtering. And

I didn't want to argue right then, or even have a discussion.

So I did what he asked. I trusted him to make five-star blueberry pancakes.

Really fast.

Nineteen

EVEN AS I WAS walking down the shoreline with Brendan, I was asking myself what I was doing. But what was the harm? And to be honest, I was hungry and five-star blueberry pancakes sounded pretty good.

Shep Martin's place was new but homey. The kitchen had tall windows and skylights, spanking-clean marble counters, hardwood floors. Acoustic jazz was playing (someone great singing "Stagger Lee"). And the pancakes *were* excellent. Not gummy, not burned, not dry. They were *jusssst* right.

Unfortunately, it was turning out to be a little awkward between Brendan and me. He said that he'd gone onto the *Trib* website to re-read some of my old columns. He'd been touched by my kidnapped child story, and my survey "Who would you rather be stranded with on a desert island — your spouse or your cat?" made him laugh out loud.

I nodded pleasantly but didn't really give much of a response. It was starting to feel a little uncomfortable for me. I didn't want to be there any longer, but I didn't know how to make a graceful exit.

As we finished the pancakes, Brendan told me that he was a radiologist and that he lived in South Bend, Indiana. I said that was great — a one-word answer.

He shook his head, seemed puzzled. "I don't usually talk about myself," he said. "I guess all this fresh air is working on me. I'm taking a sabbatical. You can sit in the dark looking at X-rays for only so long before you want to go off screaming in search of some sunlight."

I really had stayed longer than I'd meant to. I had planned to eat and run. Finally I thanked Brendan for breakfast, then headed back to Sam's. It was all I could do not to run.

I walked east a hundred yards along the path at the edge of the lake, until I reached the foot of Sam's long front lawn.

The girls greeted me with little meows, and we climbed uphill toward the house, taking the path beside my grandmother's perennial border. Sam did so many things well, didn't she? Except maybe find the right husband. And God only knew what else was coming in the letters.

She had planted a lavish three hundred feet of flowering plants that ran the length of the property from the lake almost to the road. The border was already at its summer peak. Antique pink and red shrub roses exulted; irises fluttered like flights of blue-birds on their stems.

Then I noticed that someone else was in the garden, a man, and I found myself grinning. "Hey, *you*," I called.

Twenty

~

"HENRY! It's so good to see you," I said to the tall, wiry man who was taking gardening tools out of a pickup truck. His hair was a snowy semicircle around a balding pate, his bright eyes sparkled, and he moved with more agility than you'd expect from a man in his mid-seventies.

"Jennifer, I was hoping I'd see you," he said. "I missed you at the hospital by a couple of minutes yesterday. You look beautiful, sweetheart." Then Henry gave me a big kiss and a hug that might have left a permanent impression.

I told him what I knew from that morning's call to the hospital — that Sam was the same. Henry nodded and I saw the pain in his eyes. I was remembering all the times I'd seen him and Sam putting the garden through its paces.

Henry Bullock had trained at Wisley in England and was Lake Geneva's resident master gardener. Sam was an obsessive amateur. But Henry always bragged that "Sam has a great eye. She's a great partner."

"I almost died myself when I found her on the kitchen floor," he told me, shaking his head as if he didn't want the memory in there.

"You found her?" I asked in surprise.

"I did," he answered, touching a handkerchief to his eyes. "I wish Sam could see her border this morning."

My God, his pain brought back mine. I hugged him again, and we murmured assurances to each other that Sam would be home soon. Henry had always seemed like a part of our family.

Moments later, a machine chatter made our conversation just about impossible.

Joseph, one of Henry's sons, had started up the mower in the front yard. I said goodbye, then mounted the porch steps.

My watch read twenty to nine, and I figured I had time to read a couple more letters before I went to see Sam.

Twenty-one

~

Dear Jennifer,

I want to ramble on a little about the importance of second, and even third, chances. I was helping out in the library one day when a bookmark fell from the pages of a novel. Actually, it was a hand-written note, a quote attributed to a Father Alfred D'Souza. D'Souza had written: "For a long time it had seemed to me that life was about to begin — real life. But there was always some obstacle in the way, something to be got through first, some unfinished business, time still to be served, a debt to be paid. Then life would begin. At last it dawned on me that these obstacles were my life."

Jennifer, that's how I felt as my life creaked forward. I know that I always put up a cheerful front, but that's how I felt inside.

More than twenty years had passed since I'd sworn I'd give myself a second chance and still I hadn't done it. I'd raised two wonderful daughters. I'd made about ten thousand dinners, thirty thousand beds, Brownie trooped and PTA'd and lawyer-wived my heart out. But I was resigned to my marriage with Charles, and you know what? I no longer believed that a second chance was really possible.

That little quote moved me.

And maybe it prepared me for one of the most important moments in my life.

I was only forty-three, but I had been married for nearly twenty-six years. My children had grown, and I felt that my spirit was drying up like a bug in a web in the corner of a dusty room. Jennifer, I had never really been in love. Isn't that something?

Three weeks after reading that note at the library, I met someone. I won't tell his real name, Jennifer. Not even to you.

I called him Doc.

Twenty-two

~

Jennifer dear,

If this blows your mind a little, and it should, imagine how it blew mine. KA-BOOM! Rockets to the moon!

Let me tell you how it happened. Actually, Doc and I had known each other for years, but the night I began to really know him was at an endless dinner for the Red Cross at the Hotel Como. We happened to be seated at the same table, and once we began to talk that night, we never wanted to stop. I can't even put it into words, but soon I was glowing. I was feeling something again, too. I think the electricity between us straightened my curls right to

94

the ends. I could have talked to him all
night, right into the morning. We even
made a joke about doing just that.

Of course Charles never noticed a thing.

I remember exactly what Doc was wearing that night: a beige linen suit, with a
blue oxford shirt, and a hand-painted blue
tie. He was slender and tall, with thick
blond hair streaked with silver, easily the
most handsome man in the room (in my
eyes, anyway). Over dinner, he told me
about the stars, in particular about a
comet that was about to cross our patch
of the universe and wouldn't appear again
for two hundred years. He knew about all
sorts of things, and he was passionate
about life, which I loved and had been
missing for years.

We had many common interests, but
electricity aside, I felt comfortable with
him. Immediately. He liked to listen, and
for some reason I felt I could trust him to
accept who I really was. Jen, for that night
anyway, I felt that I was home. For the first

time in twenty-five years I almost felt like myself again. Can you imagine what that's like? Actually, I hope that you can't.

I should tell you why you've never heard of Doc until now. It isn't his real name, but it suited him perfectly (because he looks *nothing* like a Doc), and I loved calling him a name that was just ours. It was one of our "secrets" — one of many, as it turns out.

We saw each other several times that summer, accidentally and accidentally on purpose, and I think we were a little in love before we knew enough to admit it. I think I fell for him first, but he wasn't far behind, and he fell as hard and as far as I did.

Jennifer, I know how terribly sad you still are about Danny. I understand as much as anyone can. And no one can tell you how long to grieve. I just want to tell you this one important thing. Don't shut out love for good. I couldn't feel this more strongly, my sweet, sweet, smart, smart girl. It's why I'm writing these letters to you.

Please don't shut out love — it's the best thing about life.

Now, stop reading right here. Think about what I'm telling you. These letters aren't just about my life, Jen; they're about yours.

PART TWO

Young Love

Twenty-three

~

I WAS SETTLING into the quite wonderful ebb and flow of life on Lake Geneva, and I was loving it even more than I thought I would.

Sam's friends were there for me at every turn. I could have eaten at somebody's home every night if I'd wanted to. In many ways, I was on summer vacation. Except that, of course, Sam was sick, and I didn't know if she would get better.

Early one afternoon I sat in her kitchen, an old-fashioned black phone cord connecting my laptop to the Internet. My e-mail inbox was crammed with notes from readers, many of whom said they missed me and hoped I was okay.

I absolutely love this connection to my readers. It's one of the best things about my job. Actually, keeping my job depends on it. If readers react to me emotionally, they buy the *Trib*. So an hour ago my editor and I agreed that I'd write from Lake Geneva for now; 750 words per column, three columns a week, just like always. Only completely different.

I opened my word-processing program and was fooling around with a couple of ideas, but my thoughts kept drifting to Sam. And I thought about my mom, who should've been there but wasn't. My mom, who shouldn't have died but had. And I thought about Danny, of course. He was always on my mind, or not far from it. And then I stopped thinking about the past. I just had to.

A light tapping on the back screen door broke into my thoughts. I went to the door and discovered Brendan Keller standing there. I hadn't seen him in a couple of days and was surprised to see him now.

He smiled and asked, "Can you come out and play?"

Twenty-four

~

"OKAY," I said, probably surprising both of us. Then, before either of us could change our mind, I stepped outside. I wasn't in the mood to write, anyway — or rather, to stare at a blank computer screen.

"Double-chocolate thick shake," Brendan said, and I immediately knew what he had in mind.

"Daddy Maxwell's," I said, and smiled.

Daddy Maxwell's Arctic Circle Diner is a white stucco, igloo-shaped local eatery at the highest level of low cuisine. It has blue-striped awnings, and what it lacks in class, it makes up for in really good food. Just two miles from Knollwood Road, it took all of three minutes to get there.

Nothing seemed to have changed since we were kids and Maxwell's was the place to be seen. We took a table by a window and turned our attention to Marie, Daddy Maxwell's latest perky waitress. She took our order, then disappeared into the kitchen.

Less than ten minutes later, I was staring over my veggie burger at Brendan's plate. He'd ordered the special of the day. Plus a chocolate thick shake. The special was a scrumptious-looking southern omelette made of three eggs wrapped around grilled onions, "dirty" fried potatoes, and extra cheddar cheese.

"You're a *doctor*," I said.

"You only go around once." Brendan grinned. "Show some guts, Jennifer. Give it a try. The omelette *and* the shake."

I laughed, reached my fork over to his plate, and lifted a bite of steaming omelette to my mouth. Then I had another bite.

And a sip of the chocolate thick shake.

Then Brendan ordered me my own omelette and shake.

"You're too thin, anyway," he said, which was one of the more endearing remarks I'd heard recently.

We lingered over the meal, and then coffee. I was surprised that I was kind of enjoying myself. We were filling each other in on our headlines of the past twenty-five years. I told him a few details about Danny, but he already knew. Brendan told me that he'd been divorced for a year and a half — his ex-wife had been having an affair with a partner in her law firm. "Figures, that ma belle Michelle would get involved at the office," he said. "Workaholic that she was — is, whatever."

I nodded, then had a guilty thought about how Danny had called me a workaholic, and he'd been right. I felt a curtain of sadness drop. Brendan noticed, and he touched my hand. I told him I was okay.

Reflexively, I pulled my hand away. So maybe I wasn't okay.

"I have to get back," I said.

"Sure," said Brendan. "Let's go."

Once we were in the car, I told Brendan that I had another deadline and would probably be working half the night.

"I get it," he said, and smiled. "Buzz off."

"No, no, nothing like that," I said. "It's just, well, buzz off." Which got a laugh out of him.

We said good-bye in the parking area of Sam's yard, and I immediately went for a twenty-minute run through the twisty streets around Knollwood. I still weigh the same 130 pounds I did in college and I wanted to keep it that way, even though Brendan said I was too thin.

I thought a little about him as I ran. He was pretty funny. And definitely smart. He also listened when I talked, and most men don't. But there had to be secrets, issues, *baggage*. What was he really doing there at the lake? Still recovering from his divorce? The truth was that he was too good-looking and charming and nice to be up there by himself.

When I got back to the house, I stood under the showerhead, letting the hot water beat down on my overactive mind. Then I dressed in shorts and a tank top, made iced tea, and took a few of Sam's letters out to the back porch.

I sat cross-legged on the floorboards, and as sunshine pinned me to the spot, I opened another envelope that had my name neatly inscribed on it.

Twenty-five

~

Dear Jen,

When you were a little girl, and so adorably cute and sweet that you could give me a toothache, you used to cry so hard when the summer was over. Every summer. Until I hit upon a plan to make it all better for you.

On the last day of summer, I would give you a big Hellmann's mayonnaise jar and send you down to the shore to "bring the beach home" with you to Madison.

I knew you'd remember and treasure those smooth, fist-size gray-and-black stones you found when walking barefoot in the shallows. And the pale rounded

pebbles that had washed up to the shoreline. And, of course, there was the sand
and the cold, clear water of Lake Geneva.
It was fascinating to watch you try to fit
your whole summer into a mayo jar.

It took several tries over one long
morning in late August — "Grandma Sam,
is it full yet?" — but you finally figured out
that the way to fit in the best of your haul
was to put the big rocks into the jar first.
After that, the pebbles and snail shells
would sift down into the spaces between
the rocks.

When the jar looked filled to the brim,
you could still get in a few lids of sand.

And finally, when there didn't seem to
be room for another thing, you dunked
your jar in the lake and topped off your
"beach" with water. Smart girl!

And I told you, Jenny, that living life was
like putting the beach into a jar. The point
wasn't to fit everything in; it was to attend
to the most important things first — the
big, beautiful rocks — the most valuable

people and experiences — and fit the lesser things in around them.

Otherwise, the best things might get left out.

I've been thinking about big rocks and how much my priorities have changed over the years. What used to be most important to me was pleasing other people; your grandfather and my mother-in-law, to name two. Going to dinner parties and having a house clean enough to stand up to a Sir Charles military inspection, to name two more.

Now that I please myself, my priorities are better. The people I love. My health. Getting the most I can out of every day. The actor Danny Kaye used to say, "Life is a great big canvas. Throw all the paint you can at it." I like that thought. More important, I try to live by it as much as I can.

I get up really early most mornings so I can watch the sun rise. I put flower buds in a lot of little bottles around the house so I can see the blossoms open everywhere. I feed whole peanuts to the blue jays because they love having their food gift-wrapped, and I never tire of watching them try to fit more than one peanut into their bills at a time. I read good, *hard* books, and if I can't sleep, I might throw a few logs onto the fire and watch *Law and Order* reruns.

And here's something I love to do. Once a month I make a huge bowl of pasta and red sauce and invite my friends who live alone to a potluck supper. They like the company over a home-cooked meal. We laugh hard and often, and they don't gossip about me too much in the car on the way home!

And in case you're wondering, Doc always comes to the potluck supper. The others just don't know that he's Doc.

Twenty-six

Dear Jen,

Here's a good laugh for us to share.

I've just come back from an afternoon in town and realized that the hem of my skirt was caught up in the waistband of my panty hose for the whole trip. I'd been to the grocery store, the hardware store, Daddy Maxwell's — with my tail feathers blowing in the breeze the whole day. No one said a word. *What a hoot!* So here's a thought that I like very much, Jen, and it took me a while to get it right. If you're going to look back on something and laugh about it, you might as well laugh about it now.

Things are almost never as bad as they first seem. Loosen up, girlfriend! You're very funny in your columns in the *Chicago Tribune*. But it seems to me that you could giggle a little more in real life. I read somewhere that the act of laughing releases some nice chemical into your brain. You feel good, and it's free!

Twenty-seven

~

I LAUGHED at Sam's letter, and then I
wasn't laughing. Tears were rolling down
my cheeks. I missed her so much, I almost
couldn't stand it. Visiting her twice a day at
the hospital wasn't enough. Reading her
letters made me want to hear the sound of
her voice, even if it was just one more
time. I needed to talk to Sam about some
things.

Like, who was Doc? Did I know him? Was
he still alive, and if he was, wouldn't he be
visiting Sam at the hospital? Had I seen him
there?

I remembered trying to stuff Lake Geneva into a mayo jar when I was five or so.

But that Sam not only remembered but found it so meaningful had cracked me up, and choked me up, too.

I walked down to the lake and toed up a beautiful black stone with a few rough edges. I brought it back and put it on the growing pile of Sam's mail on the coffee table.

Right next to my laptop, which was humming softly, waiting for me to start writing.

You have a day job, Jennifer.

The first thing I did was to dump the column I'd started that morning. I had a new idea, but for a long while I didn't know where to start.

Finally I wrote:

The last time I saw my Grandma Sam at her house on Lake Geneva, we were saying good-bye at the end of a beautiful Labor Day weekend.

Sam looked healthy and happy, but as she hugged me, I got the feeling that something was on her mind and maybe she didn't know how to tell me. The moment passed, and I didn't ask her about it.

I got into the car and honked a little salute as I reached the end of her driveway. How could I have known that the next time I'd see my grandmother, she would be in a coma and that maybe she would never be able to talk to me again.

As I chiseled my column, the day disappeared into night. At one in the morning, I was still writing and rewriting about how lucky I was that Sam had put her thoughts down for me to read. How many of my readers were so lucky? How many of us know the true stories of our parents and grandparents? How many of us share the stories of our lives with our own children? What a loss to the children if we don't. What are we but our stories?

Writing the column was like unraveling a sweater. I tugged on a thought and the words came free in a smooth, untangled line. I completely overshot the 750-word limit on my first draft and had to cut and rewrite and cut again.

When the piece was as good as I could make it, I ended it by inviting my readers to tell me stories about their loved ones. I was already anticipating the mail I'd get, the stories I'd be privileged to read, the family secrets that would be shared with me.

At 2:00 in the morning, just before I went blind from staring into the computer screen, I pressed the SEND button. A microsecond later, my story was in Debbie's electronic mailbox at the *Trib.*

Then I went to bed and cried into my pillow. I wasn't sad, not at all. It was just so beautiful to have an intense feeling and the right words at the same time.

What are we but our stories?

Twenty-eight

~

I WOKE UP excited and kind of happy. My column was written — it was about as good as I could do — and I had the day off. Yippee!

My blue swimsuit was still inside the duffel bag, where I'd packed it back in Chicago. I put on the one-piece with the scooped neckline and quickly did a few chores. Then I did something completely unexpected. I went looking for Brendan.

His uncle's house was sparkling in the morning sun, the light glinting off all that glass. Behind the house, the lake was calm and glistening.

I knocked on the kitchen door, but there was no answer. I finally cupped my hands and peered between them through the window.

I felt a little disappointed, I guess, because Brendan wasn't around, and I wanted to play.

Then I saw him through the living-room window, and when I looked more closely, I was floored. Brendan was on his knees in the middle of the rug, his hands folded in front of him.

He was praying.

Twenty-nine

~

TOTALLY EMBARRASSED, I turned away and walked off the porch and across the lawn unnoticed. Suddenly the kitchen door whined open and slammed closed behind me. I looked around to see Brendan coming toward me. *Oh no. Busted.*

"Hey, Jen. I thought I heard somebody knock. You up for a swim?" he called.

"Umm, sure," I said.

He flashed me a grin — a beauty, nothing self-conscious about it. Then he yelled a goofy challenge about rotten eggs and sprinted toward the lake.

So I did the most instinctive thing — I took off behind him. I raced down the lawn and then thirty feet of white-painted dock, and when I got to the end of it, I cannonballed into the water. Just do it, right?

I smacked bottom first into the lake, came back up, and started stroking behind Brendan, who was headed toward a channel marker about fifty or sixty yards out. I raced to win. But Brendan was a very good swimmer, and to his credit, he beat my pants off.

He grinned. "So who's a rotten egg, you rotten egg!"

The two of us hung on to the buoy bobbing in the wake of a particularly noisy motorboat zipping around the lake. I squinted through wet eyelashes at Brendan. I'm a pretty good swimmer, but the recent smoking hadn't helped my time, and Brendan's freestyle was awesome.

"You could have let me win," I said. "Or get a little closer."

He shrugged. "Winning is overrated in this country. It was a great swim, though."

"I think you're right," I said. "And mornings at the lake are underrated." The temperature of the water was just about perfect, and the sun was warm on my face and shoulders.

"I'm starting to *really* remember you now, Scout. You were stuck-up and totally impressed with yourself."

No kidding? I must've had him fooled back in the day. "Still am," I told him, splashing water in his face. "Hey," I said, grinning up into his eyes. "I think I've got an idea."

Brendan looked momentarily confused. "For another column?"

Thirty

~

"DO YOU WANT to go sailing?" I asked.

"*You? Sailing?* Aren't you swamped with work?"

"Actually, I just wrote one of my better pieces in a while."

"Champagne!" Brendan cried.

"One step at a time."

Now here's what I was beginning to discover about Brendan. He'd grown up to be a really nice person — interesting, fun, and not self-involved, as far as I could tell. Not only did he encourage me to talk about Sam as much as I needed to, he was thoughtful in other ways. For instance, he made the sandwiches for our impromptu outing and brought me a long-billed cap to wear so that I wouldn't get burned. Pretty sweet, actually.

Right off, I could tell that the years Brendan had spent landlocked in Indiana hadn't compromised his skill as a sailor. He rigged his uncle's scow in ten minutes flat and got the boat away from the dock on the first try.

Scows are top-heavy, flat-bottomed sailboats, fast and unstable, as I well knew from all the summers I'd spent racing up and down the seven-mile-long lake in my grandfather's sixteen-footer. Brendan manned the mainsail while I dropped the centerboard into the well and took charge of the jib, our movements meshing as if we'd been sailing together for a while.

It was such a tremendous day to be out on the water. A cooling breeze gusted under a hazy sun, and the air was a perfect seventy-five degrees.

Brendan commented on the beautiful, historic homes lining the lakeshore. He hadn't seen them for so long, he felt as though he were seeing them for the first time. The pleasant thoughts were cut off abruptly by the roar of a Jet Ski as a pair of teenagers rode circles around us, swamping our boat. I reached for the jib line, and Brendan scrambled to the high side — but it was too late.

The boat capsized, dumping the two of us into the drink.

"You okay?" I heard as I sputtered to the surface.

"Fine. You?"

"Yep. Don't worry. I got the little bastard's plate number."

I laughed as Brendan righted the scow and helped me back in. Soon we were sailing again, soaking wet but otherwise okay. The rest of the afternoon was a very nice blur. We sailed through the Narrows, passing the Lake Geneva Country Club and Black Point, an eccentric-looking, thirteen-bedroom summer "cottage" built at the end of the nineteenth century. When our faces were stiff from sun and wind, we sailed back to Knollwood Road — to change our clothes.

Brendan had asked me out to dinner.

And I had accepted.

Thirty-one

~

I HAD JUST the right dress hanging in my closet: a simple black shift that set off my sun-pinked skin. *This isn't a date,* I told myself as I put on makeup, but not too much. *It's a reunion. A chat between old friends.*

"Wow. Look at you!" Brendan said as he arrived to pick me up for . . . whatever it was supposed to be.

"And look at you!" I said. He had on pressed jeans and a blue cashmere sweater, loafers, no socks, and he was tan.

"Your very own beach bum," he said, and winked.

"You look great."

"It's the loafers," he quipped.

We had dinner on the dockside terrace of the French Country Inn, with a candle sputtering on the table between us and the lake bumping up against the pilings. We were still catching up over braised breast of duckling and wild rice when Brendan said a few words about his folks and asked about mine. I told him that neither of my parents was still alive. "It's just Sam and me," I said.

"I'm sorry about your folks. And everything else that's happened to you."

"It's okay. Anyway, here we are on the lake again."

By the time coffee was served, we had moved on to lighter subjects. We joked and laughed and were still so in sync, it surprised me a lot. I had expected dead spots in the conversation, but there hadn't been many. When they happened, it was mostly me being too guarded.

Then the dinner was over and it was time to go home. That's when I realized, or maybe admitted to myself, that I *was* on a date. The best date I'd had in quite a while, actually.

Thirty-two

~

IT CERTAINLY hadn't been planned that way, but Brendan and I had been together nearly the whole day. And now there was an awkward moment at the front door. We were standing close enough that I could smell the cologne he used. *I need to stop this nonsense right now,* I told myself. *For both of our sakes.*

I caught my breath as that notion flashed through my mind. Then I put the brakes on any fantasy that could lead to the kind of trouble I couldn't handle. I stepped back away from Brendan.

"Well, I'd ask you in for coffee," I said,

"but I should start writing my column for tomorrow."

"Okay," Brendan said. But then he sat down on the porch steps, and he showed no sign of leaving.

"Come swimming with me, or just sit out here and shoot the breeze for a little while more. Anything you want. Just don't work tonight. You don't need to work. Come on, Jenny. Loosen up."

The words *Jenny, loosen up* stung a little. But I was also struck by the choice of words. Sam had said almost the same thing in one of her letters.

"Okay," I said. "But you can't ever call me 'Jenny.' Danny called me Jenny."

"I'm sorry. So talk to me, Scout. You've hardly talked about him at all."

"Sometime I will. Maybe. But not tonight," I said. "I'll talk about Danny when I'm ready." Danny and other things.

He seemed confused, or troubled.

I settled down on the porch steps beside Brendan. "What?" I asked.

"Oh, it's nothing. I just wanted to tell somebody that I quit my job," Brendan finally said, pulling on his lower lip. "I quit today."

My head rocked back a little. "You quit your job? Why? What happened, Brendan?"

"Nothing too dramatic. I've been looking at shadows on sheets of plastic for too long. I was thinking it's time to get a few priorities straight," he said. Then he gave me a dead-on look that grabbed and held me.

I glanced away reflexively. The moonlight cast a pale glow over the lake. Peepers and crickets chirped in the bushes. We were sitting very close to each other. Too close.

"I really have to go in," I said. I stood up from the porch steps. "Thanks for the day. It was fun."

Brendan stood, too. He was physically imposing, and he *was* handsome. He leaned in and kissed my forehead, which was oddly nice. Then he gave me his best smile. "Good night, Jennifer. I had a good time, too."

Soon I was in my bed, the same one I'd slept in for years at the lake. A cup of spearmint tea was on the night table. I stared at the ceiling, and some strange, conflicting thoughts swirled in my head. *Brendan and I had a nice night*, I thought. *And that's the end of it. Why? Because it is, that's why.*

I opened another letter from Sam.

Thirty-three

Jennifer,

Nothing much worth writing about happened between Doc and me at first. Almost no touching, not even a lingering look in town. It was complicated. His wife had died a few years before, but I was certainly married, and with children, though they were grown. Doc still had children at home. There was one remarkable moment that first summer, and it became a touchstone for us.

One night when your grandfather was having dinner after golf with his pals at Medinah outside Chicago (or so Charles told me), Doc used some connections to get us into the Yerkes Observatory. Yerkes was strictly a scientific observatory back then, home to the largest refracting telescope in the world and not open to the public. At night, no one would be there.

So imagine the two of us sneaking across the parklike lawns, briefly holding hands, approaching the Yerkes complex of buildings with the three huge domes silhouetted against the summer night sky. Then we climbed the wide steps and entered the most beautiful marble halls I have ever seen.

Doc had a flashlight and we followed the beam up the back staircase until we reached a door that opened into the largest of the domes. I was stunned by how large it was inside, like a sports stadium in the round. A telescope in the center pointed up through a slit in the dome to the cobalt sky beyond.

"Watch this, Samantha. You won't believe it," he said. "Ready?"

"I think so." I wasn't really sure.

He pulled a lever, and the floor we were standing on — at least seventy feet across — began to lift us upward. Suddenly we could actually look into the fixed eyepiece of the telescope.

It was Friday, the beginning of the weekend, and I knew that Charles would be driving up from Chicago soon. Still, Doc and I dared to stay in the cavernous dome for over an hour. The stars were dazzling, as if the universe was putting on a display just for us. He talked about the fact that what we were watching in the sky had actually happened hundreds of years before, and then Doc admitted how long he'd secretly wished to be alone with me like this.

"I wished for it, too," I confessed. Wished, prayed, fantasized, almost every day since the Red Cross dinner.

We kissed under all those billions of twinkling stars. Then we kissed again, longer and harder. But that was it. There we stood, two people falling in love but separated by my marriage, our families, but especially his children, who were still at home with Doc.

He eventually drove me to the corner of Knollwood Road — and *didn't* kiss me when I got out of the car, though, God, I wanted him to. I entered the house and found that Charles was sleeping. I had hoped I wasn't going to have to make up a story, but I shouldn't have worried.

I undressed quietly, and when I was under the sheets, I looked into Charles's face. To my surprise, I didn't feel any guilt about my adventure with Doc that night — but I did have an interesting thought. I wondered if Charles would notice anything different about me in the morning. *Would he notice that while he slept, I'd become happy?*

Thirty-four

~

WHEN I ANSWERED the phone by my bed, it was barely 6:40 A.M. and I got a surprise that I wasn't prepared for. Brendan spoke into my ear. "Wake up, Jennifer. The lake is calling."

I wasn't sure what I was doing, but I began to smile and then I put my bathing suit on. I felt like a kid again, and it was good. I felt free.

Outside, I joined Brendan in a jog that turned into a full run to the lake. Finally both of us were screaming his semimaniacal war whoop, which actually made all the sense in the world. The water was freezing, fricking cold at that hour.

"It's not even seven," I sputtered as I did a stiff, chilly breaststroke beside him.

"Perfect time for a swim. I have a new mantra: 'Live every day from the crack of dawn until I can't keep my eyes open a second longer.'"

Okay. Who can fault a philosophy like that, especially since his spirit *was* contagious. We swam over to Sam's dock and hauled ourselves up. He shook off some water, then rolled onto his back. I did the same, and lying next to each other, we stared up at the morning sky. It *was* perfect, actually.

"Takes you back," I said.

"Or maybe forward," he mumbled under his breath.

I was aware that my right side from shoulder to ankle was touching Brendan's left side. The pressure made my body tingle, but I didn't move.

When he turned his face toward me, I avoided his eyes. So he put his hand on my waist and pulled me even closer. I wasn't expecting it, but the heat that flashed through my body almost melted my swimsuit.

And then Brendan kissed me on the lips. A good, long kiss, a really nice one.

And I kissed him back.

And neither of us said a word, which was exactly the right thing to do.

Thirty-five

~

FROM THE MORNING of the kiss, Brendan and I spent more and more of our time together. To be perfectly honest, I knew exactly what this was — a sweet, fleeting summer romance. And so did he, I was sure. We hadn't even "done anything," as the popular saying goes.

Brendan and I launched most mornings with a swim; then we took turns making breakfast, sometimes including his uncle Shep in the ritual. And we visited Sam every day before noon; then I would go again, usually about seven. I always talked to Sam, sometimes for hours at a time. I told her what was going on in my life and asked questions about her letters.

On one particular day, I waited outside Sam's room while Dr. Brendan Keller and Dr. Max Weisberg conferred. When they found me in the hallway, Brendan had a serious expression on his face. He saw me looking, though, and brushed the look aside.

I'll admit I'd been hoping for a little good news. Maybe I thought that because I was reading Sam's letters and hearing her voice and seeing her so vividly in my mind, she would get better, she had to get better. But now I thought, *She isn't going to get better. I can see it in their eyes. They just don't want to tell me.*

"She's a strong lady," Brendan said, and put his hand over my arm. "She's hanging in there pretty well, Jen. Maybe there's a reason for that."

When we left the hospital, Brendan tried to cheer me up. I liked that he was sensitive to my needs, and I also sensed what a good doctor he must be. Why had he quit his job, though?

He said, "How'd you like to go on a road trip? It'll be fun."

Well, it *was* a glorious day for a drive. So with the CD player blasting James Taylor's and Aretha's and Ella Fitzgerald's greatest hits, we took a route that skirted Chicago, bringing us into South Bend, Indiana, just before noon.

I was in for a real treat, Brendan said, winking. A friend of his was one of the coaches for the Fighting Irish, and we had been invited to watch the Notre Dame team scrimmage down on the practice field. We sat cross-legged in the short grass while a couple of dozen top-notch bruis-ers ran their plays. Watching football on television has never moved me, but the sport has a whole different feeling up close. The speed of the action at ground level was incredible, and so was the sharp crack of contact as helmets and shoulder pads collided.

Watching the Blue and Gold was a surprisingly nice way to spend an afternoon, probably because it was Brendan's team. It was also fun to see where he lived, though he stopped short of showing me his old house, or even the apartment where he'd moved after his divorce. "It's a complete, off-limits disaster area; I'd be too embarrassed," he said. So we headed back to Lake Geneva without seeing his place. A little strange, I thought, but no big deal.

The day after our Notre Dame adventure, I had a surprise for Brendan. I took him to the Yerkes Observatory. I kept seeing parallels between him and me and Sam and Doc, so I had to go there. It was daytime and there was a crowd ringing the perimeter of the big dome, but it was still a magical place.

The whole time I kept thinking about what it had meant to Sam and Doc. And I wondered, Who is Doc, anyway? The next time I talked to Sam, she was going to give up her secret, so help me.

On another morning I arranged for Brendan and me to catch a ride on the mail boat, a double-decker ferry that scoots along the shoreline, delivering mail to the lakefront homes. That same afternoon we saw a couple of silly blockbusters at the little theater in town, one right after the other. We had another habit, too. Last thing at night, after I came back from seeing Sam, we took a long walk on the path that circles the lake.

Being with Brendan definitely felt like an old-fashioned summer romance — fast, irresistible, and probably a little dumb, but even if it was, we both seemed to feel the same way about it. I had the sense that Brendan needed it, too, and also that he was holding back, careful that this didn't get too serious.

I even called him on it while we were delivering mail on Hank Mischuk's ferry.

But Brendan just laughed. "I'm an open book, Scout. You're the mystery woman."

Then one day the strangest thing happened. I didn't turn in my column! It was the first time I'd ever done it, or rather *not* done it. I apologized to Debbie and promised to make up for it, but inside I was exultant. Something was changing, wasn't it? Maybe I was living every day "from the crack of dawn until I closed my eyes."

That morning I told Sam everything at the hospital, and even though she never said a word, I felt I knew what she wanted me to do next. It was what Sam would have done herself.

Thirty-six

~

LATE THAT AFTERNOON Brendan and I sat together at the tip of Sam's dock. I was wiggling my toes in the water. Brendan was, too.

It was time for me to tell some of my secrets to him. I wanted to do it. I was ready.

"It happened off a beach in Oahu." I spoke in a soft, low voice. "Danny liked bright lights and big cities, so if it had been up to him, we would've taken our vacation in Paris, or maybe London. We decided on Hawaii because *I* wanted to go there."

I sighed, then caught my breath. "At the last minute I got involved in a terrible kidnapping story. So Danny went on ahead of me. A couple of days later I was finally on my way from Chicago," I said. "Late that afternoon, he went out for a run — alone, of course."

Brendan was watching me intently as I managed to get the words out somehow. "You don't have to do this, Jennifer," he finally said.

"Yeah, I do. I have to do this. I need to get it out and I want to, Brendan. I want to tell you. I don't want to be a mystery woman anymore."

Brendan nodded, and he took my hand. Something had happened between the two of us in the past couple of weeks; I had come to trust Brendan more than I could have ever imagined. He was my friend. No, he was more than that.

"It was a beautiful evening on the north shore of Oahu, a place called Kahuku. I've read all the weather reports. Danny took off his T-shirt and ran down into the surf, which was high, but he was an athlete, a good swimmer. He loved to push the envelope as much as he could. That was one of his favorite sayings, 'Let's go for it, Jenny!' He was always teasing me to go for it."

I felt tears slipping down my cheeks, and I really didn't want to cry. Not in front of Brendan. "He was a good, caring person . . . and there were so many things he still wanted to do —" My voice faltered badly. I didn't know if I could finish what I'd started. "I loved him so much. . . . I *see* every minute of what happened in Hawaii. This horrible and recurring nightmare that I have. For the past year and a half, I've *watched* Danny die over and over again. He calls out to me. With his last breath, he calls my name."

I stopped to collect myself. I realized that I was squeezing Brendan's hand very tight.

"It was *my* fault, Brendan. If I had gone to Hawaii when I was supposed to, Danny would be alive today."

Brendan held my hand. "It's okay, it's okay," he whispered, his voice soft and gentle.

"There's more to it," I said so low that I could barely hear myself. "When I got back to Chicago, I couldn't stop crying and thinking about what had happened. Sam came and stayed with me. She took the best care of me, Brendan."

I couldn't talk for a minute. But I had come this far, hadn't I?

"I was in my bathroom. I felt this sharp pain, and then I was doubled over on the bathroom floor. I screamed and Sam came running. She knew immediately that I had miscarried. She held me and cried with me. I lost the baby. I lost our baby, Brendan. I was pregnant, and I lost our little 'peanut.'"

Thirty-seven

BRENDAN HELD ME for a long time on the dock. Then I had to say good night to Sam, so I drove over to the medical center about 8:30. Brendan offered to come, but I told him I was all right. I brought Sam roses from her garden.

"Sam, wake up. Look," I said, "you have to see your roses. And I need to talk to you."

But she didn't respond in any way. She couldn't even hear me, could she?

I placed the flowers in a crockery jug on the windowsill and fluffed them until they looked just right.

Then I turned back to Sam. "You're missing everything. A lot is happening, Sam."

She looked pinched and faded, not good. I'd never been more worried about losing her. Every time I saw Sam I was scared it could be the last.

I pulled a chair up close to the bed. "I've got a secret to tell you," I said. "Sam, there's someone I like at the lake. I'm trying hard not to like him too much. But he's so sweet; he's smart in a good way. He's even kind of a hunk. I know, I know, you never get all three of those qualities in the same man."

I gave Sam a moment to take in the news. "I'll call him Brendan. Ha, ha. Because that's his name. I could also call him *Doc*. He's a doctor.

"You remember how I used to follow Brendan Keller around when I was a little kid? Well, he's all grown up. I trust him completely, Sam. I told him about Danny, and the baby. I don't know how much he likes me. I mean, he definitely likes me, but he's holding back a little. I guess we both are. Confused yet? I am."

I finally stopped babbling and took one of Sam's hands and held it. I played that game where you think something and you pretend somebody else can hear your thoughts.

I need you to meet Brendan, Sam. Can you do that for me? Just this once.

Thirty-eight

~

"YOU KNOW that this is completely unreal, this life on the lake that we're living
this summer," Brendan said, and smiled. We
were driving home from dinner at the Lake
Geneva Inn the next night. It was pouring
rain, sheeting the stuff. I almost told Brendan to pull over to the side of the road.

"It was your idea — every moment from
sunup until I can't keep my eyes open any
longer. Those were *your* words," I said.

When we got to Sam's, the two of us
raced across her puddled yard to the protective wing of the front porch. I yanked
open the door.

"Stay here. I'll get towels," I said, and walked inside first.

I was halfway to the linen closet when a table lamp flickered out — I smelled something burning. Uh-oh.

I shoved the armchair away from the wall with my hip and saw a limp white rag lying in the corner.

It was Euphoria.

Something was wrong with Euphoria.

I called, "Brendan, come quick," and then he was right there beside me. He lifted my cat and gently laid her down again in the center of the carpet. What I saw made me sick. The fur around Euphoria's mouth was singed and bloody. And then I realized that she wasn't breathing.

"Oh, God, what's happened to her?"

"Looks like she bit into an electric cord," Brendan said. He placed two fingers high up against the inside fold of her left hind leg.

"She's in arrest, Jennifer. Poor thing's got no pulse."

I'd loved that little girl since I rescued her from the pound right after Danny's death. Euphoria wasn't just a cat to me. I loved her dearly. I clutched at Brendan's arm.

"Please! Can you help her?"

He took a deep breath.

"Okay, listen to me. When I say so, press right *here*. Five times." Then Brendan turned Euphoria onto her side. She made no movement on her own, no sound.

Now he opened her jaws and bent to fit his mouth to hers. Then he blew a little breath into her lungs.

Phh.

"Do it now," he told me. "Press, Jennifer."

I pressed on the left side of Euphoria's rib cage, massaging her heart, praying with mine. Then Brendan signaled me to stop. My heart was racing, thundering.

He bent over her and breathed into her mouth a second time. *Phh.* Then he had me press again. He was working very hard. Being a doctor right before my eyes.

Then I got to see a miracle happen. I *felt*

Euphoria come back to life under my hands. She quivered and coughed. Then she opened her beautiful green eyes and looked up at me. Her eyes were filled with love. She was breathing on her own.

She finally wobbled to her feet and said, "Yow."

I grabbed her up in one arm and kissed her. I threw my other arm around Brendan's neck and kissed him. I hugged him hard, almost crushing Euphoria between us. "You saved my baby," I whispered.

Brendan sat back on his heels, a look of complete satisfaction on his face. Then he said a very cool thing.

"You gotta know I love you, Jennifer. I just gave the kiss of life to a cat."

I stared into his eyes with amazement — Brendan had just said *I love you*.

Thirty-nine

~

IT WAS OCCURRING to me lately that the summer was going too quickly. It was the "magic hour" again — our favorite time to be out on Sam's dock. Brendan and I were sitting side by side, dangling our feet, leaning into each other. I noticed that he was staring out across the lake, lost in his thoughts, wherever it was that they took him.

"You okay?" I asked. I knew that he was, of course. How could he not be?

"I . . . uh . . . ," he said. And then Brendan didn't say anything.

159

"*You're* at a loss for words? I can't believe it. I *don't* believe it. You . . . uh . . . what?" I kidded.

But he didn't joke back for once. What was this? Was it time for Brendan to share a few secrets, too? Did he trust me enough?

"I have to tell you something, Jennifer," he said.

I turned my shoulder so that it wasn't touching his anymore. I could see his face better now. Brendan was averting his eyes.

"You're not going to tell me that you're still married?" I asked, and didn't like those words as they came out of my mouth.

He looked at me. "I'm divorced, Jennifer. That's not it. . . . The problem is that when we met a couple of weeks ago, I had no idea that any of this was going to happen. Who could have? I had no idea there was somebody like you out there."

"What a shame, buddy," I said. "I feel pretty bad for you."

But Brendan didn't laugh. If anything, he

looked worried. Not like himself. Now I got it. He was falling for me. "But . . ."

I had a feeling that I wasn't going to like *but*. I was so sure of it that my body went cold.

"But *what?*" I asked.

Forty

~

HE DIDN'T ANSWER my question right away, and my insides continued to churn. Whatever was happening, it wasn't good. Brendan wouldn't, or couldn't, look me in the eye, and he'd never been like that before.

"Brendan, what is it?"

He sighed. "This is going to be hard. I think I'm going to have to back into it."

"Okay," I said. "Just tell me what's going on."

He held out his wrist. "Have I ever shown you this, Jennifer?"

It was a handsome Rolex watch. Of course I'd noticed it before, but he hadn't said anything about the watch.

"Kind of fancy for you," I said.

"It was a gift from a friend who used to live next door to me in Indiana. His name was John Kearney. John was a professor at Notre Dame. Very, very nice guy. Four kids, all girls. We used to go to football games together, play tennis once a week. When he was fifty-one, he went to his doctor about a little cough and came back with an X-ray showing a large spot on his lung," Brendan said.

"He showed it to me. When I saw the film, I got John into the Mayo Clinic, where I had interned. I found him a top surgeon. Oncologist. Jennifer, six months later, John weighed a hundred and ten pounds. He couldn't eat and couldn't get out of bed. He was in constant pain and he wasn't getting any better."

Brendan looked into my eyes. I was touched by the depth of his sadness. I had been there myself; maybe I was still there.

"I was going to take John in for another radiation treatment, but he flat out refused.

He said, 'Please stop this, Brendan. I love you and I know you mean well. But I've had a good life. I have four beautiful daughters. I don't want to be like this. Please let me go.'

"I apologized and I hugged him, and then both of us cried. I knew John was right. I couldn't change what I'd already done, but the way I viewed the aggressive measures that doctors sometimes take, because we *can,* changed forever.

"When he died, John left me his watch," Brendan said. "What it means to me is 'quality time,' making the best of it. So when I read my own CAT scan at the beginning of the summer, I decided to do what's best for me. I'm sorry about this. I can't tell you how sorry. I don't like melodrama very much, especially when it's happening to me. I'm dying, Jennifer."

Forty-one

~

I MAY HAVE blacked out for a second or two. I heard Brendan say "my own CAT scan" but I'm not completely sure I grasped what came after that. Then he said, and I heard this very clearly, "There's nothing that can be done for me. Believe me, I've examined every possibility."

I felt this incredible core of pain at the center of my chest, or maybe where my heart *used* to be. I was dizzy and nauseous and I couldn't really believe what I knew I'd just heard. Everything around me on the dock seemed fuzzy and unreal. The water I had my feet in, my own body, Brendan's hand resting on mine. Suddenly I reached out and held him as tightly as I could. I kissed his cheek, the side of his forehead. I felt so incredibly sad, and empty.

"Tell me what's wrong," I finally said.

"Well, it's called glioblastoma multi-forme, Jennifer. Big name for a bad cancer that I have right *here*." He pointed his finger to the back and side of his head, just behind his left ear. He explained that he'd looked at his own case over and over, consulted experts from as far away as London, and kept arriving at the same unfortunate conclusion.

"The only treatment for this form of cancer is experimental, extremely radical," he told me. "Surgery is a nightmare. The risk of paralysis is phenomenal. They probably can't get all of the cells, anyway. The cancer usually keeps coming back, even with radiation and chemo."

Tears were rolling down my face, and I felt hollow. "This isn't true," I whispered.

"I didn't know how to tell you, Jennifer. I still don't." He pulled me into his arms, and

I let Brendan hold me. When he spoke again, his voice was low and measured. "I'm so, so sorry, Jennifer." He was soothing *me*. "I'm sorry."

"Oh, Brendan," I whispered. "How can this be happening?"

"A little quality time. That's all I wanted," he said in the softest whisper. "That's why I decided to have a last summer up here. And then I found you again, Scout."

Forty-two

~

BRENDAN AND I hadn't even been to bed together, and now maybe I understood why. It was one of the few things that I did understand at that point.

"I don't want to be alone tonight," I said against his cheek. "Is that okay?"

Then Brendan gave me that incandescent grin of his. "I didn't want to be alone for the past thirty-four nights."

"But who's counting?"

"I am," he said.

I took Brendan's hand and kissed it. "You *were.*"

It seemed that we got from the dock to the bedroom without even touching the ground. We held on to each other inside the doorway, swaying together on the threshold. We kissed for a long moment, and I finally admitted to myself that I really loved Brendan's kisses. Then we fumbled with our clothes and fell onto the bed in my room.

"I guess my sob story worked," he cracked.

"Shhhhh. No jokes."

He couldn't resist, though. "Scout? Is it you?" he asked, and both of us started laughing again. Actually, I loved laughing with him, loved that he could make me laugh.

I put my hands in Brendan's thick hair and kissed him over and over. I loved the sensation of his skin rubbing against mine. I loved his smell. I touched the soft curls on his chest, then ran my hands down the length of his body. I was taking him all in, learning about him. I wanted to consume Brendan, and in every way that I could, I did. I couldn't deny my feelings anymore. I didn't want to.

Brendan tenderly kissed my breasts, the hollow of my throat, my mouth, my eyelids; then he did it all over again. I was completely lost. He was so gentle and good. He murmured my name, his hands gliding over my body. He had a wonderful touch, and it gave me goose bumps.

"You're beautiful without your clothes on, even more beautiful than I imagined," he said. It was very nice to hear, just the right thing. I doubt that he knew how much I needed to hear that. I hadn't been to bed with anybody in over a year and a half.

"So are you," I said.

"I'm beautiful?"

"Yep, you are."

We didn't hold anything back; there was no shyness, not too many first-time nerves. It was as if this had always been meant to happen. Maybe that was even true. After a while we rested in each other's arms, whispering. I couldn't stop staring into Brendan's incredible eyes.

All of my fear was gone, all of the uncertainty and doubt. Finally, we lay on our sides, facing each other, snuggled in so tight that there was no space between us. My legs were hooked around his waist, his knees tucked into mine.

That's how we slept.

When I woke up, I was still in Brendan's arms. I had to admit I liked it there.

"Scout?" he whispered, and I punched him in the arm.

"See, you're still a tomboy."

"How can you say that — after last night?"

"Right. A tom*girl*. Definitely a *girl*. No, you're a beautiful woman, Jennifer. You make me so happy."

I hugged him tightly, and just then "the crack of dawn" sliced through the part in the curtains.

Almost on cue, Brendan's eyes widened, and there was that amazing smile of his.

"We're off!" he said.

How could I possibly say no?

Not wearing any swimsuits, we ran like little kids out into the yard. A flock of startled ducks flew up through the mist that was rising off the lake as we thundered down the dock. The planks clanked and clunked beneath our bare feet.

We screamed as we dove into the crystal-clear lake.

As if everything was right with the world, instead of terribly, terribly wrong.

Forty-three

~

I VISITED SAM that morning and I had to tell her everything. In the past Sam would have said, "You're bubbling over. Slow down, Jennifer." But I couldn't slow down; there wasn't time. Still, we talked — well, I talked — for over an hour.

"Sam, I don't feel guilty anymore, and I don't much want to examine why. Maybe it's because Brendan is sick. I have to try and do something. What do you think, Grandmother? I need your help. You've been resting long enough." But Sam had nothing to say to me, and it was terribly sad and frustrating. All my life, she had always been there.

Later in the morning I had a meeting with Max Weisberg. I needed a second opinion, and not about Sam. I wanted to talk to Max about Brendan.

I followed the charming aromas of burned macaroni and coffee to the hospital coffee shop, a cafeteria-style room with Formica tables and a commanding view of the parking lot. I filled a paper cup with sugar and coffee, then turned to see Dr. Max sitting at one of the tables near the window.

I'd met with Max so many times in the past couple of weeks, he'd almost lost his power to intimidate. Actually, he looked really young, sitting across from me in his scrubs. His brush-cut blond hair was standing at attention as he polished off dry rye toast and black coffee.

"Yum," I said.

"Eat your heart out. What's up?"

I summed up what Brendan told me the night before, that he had a serious brain tumor, with a very poor prognosis, and that he'd elected to have a great summer and not to pursue any radical treatment program.

When I was finished, Max said, "When are you going to stop smoking?"

"Max. Don't. Please. Besides, I basically quit. Until yesterday."

"I mean it." He sighed. "Look, I'm not going to lie to you. GBM is a horror. Brendan is absolutely right about that. The surgery *is* dangerous; the treatment fails as often as it works. Brendan knows all of this."

"Max, can anything be done? Is there any chance he could come through this with a decent quality of life?"

"*If* he survived the experimental surgery, if he survived the treatment, he'd have a thirty percent chance of living for two to five years. But, Jennifer, he could go through the surgery and be completely paralyzed. Brendan would be able to think but not speak or do anything for himself. Believe it or not, I'm understating the risk."

I didn't want to start crying in front of

Max, but sometimes he had the bedside manner of a stun gun.

"I don't know what to do," I said. "I'm going a little crazy here. Can you tell?"

"Sorry," said Dr. Max. "My specialty is neurology."

I glared at him, tears started down my cheeks, and to my amazement, his cold demeanor melted.

"I'm sorry. That was bad," he said. "Even for me."

He put his head in his hands and his elbows on the table. "Let me say this in a better way, Jen. It sounds to me like Brendan has decided to make good use of whatever time he has left. He's chosen to have a beautiful summer with you. He's lucky to spend a summer with you, and I'm quite certain he knows it. In other words, I think he's making a very intelligent choice. I really am sorry." Then Max actually took my hands in his. "You don't deserve this, Jennifer. And neither does Brendan."

Forty-four

❧

I TURNED OVER a lot of things that Dr. Max Weisberg had said as I drove toward Sam's house. I parked the car under the oak, kicked off my loafers, and walked to Shep's dock. Brendan was out on the lake, swimming. He looked so vital — not sick, certainly not terminally ill. My stomach started to churn.

He saw me and waved. Then he called, "Come in, the water's perfect. *You* look perfect."

"No, you come," I said, patting the dock beside me. "Sit by me. I'm saving a spot. The *dock* is perfect."

Brendan swam my way. He pulled himself up in one smooth motion. Then he put his arm around me and we kissed.

"Not right now," he said after the kiss.

"Not right now, what?" I asked.

"Let's not talk about it right now, Jen," he said. He looked me in the eye, squinting on account of the sun. "It would be a waste of such a beautiful day. We have time to get into the serious stuff."

Fine. So I made lunch and served it on Sam's wide front porch: chicken salad with white grapes on eight-grain, chips, iced tea. Below us, sunlight skipped across the lake and the fragrance of Sam's roses saturated the air. Henry was working in the garden; he seemed to be there all the time.

It *was* a perfect day, wasn't it? The right guy, the right girl, only the timing was wrong. I couldn't help it, I felt as though I was going to break down and cry all through lunch, but I held it inside. Maybe Brendan was used to the idea of his dying, but I wasn't.

He was waterproofing Shep's deck and the job was only half done, so after lunch Brendan went back to work. I was clearing the table when I found a note folded under my plate. It read:

JENNIFER,
YOU ARE FORMALLY INVITED TO DINNER AT THE GUESTHOUSE.
7:00 P.M. MORE OR LESS.
COME AS SWEET AS YOU ARE.
BRENDAN

Forty-five

~

A CHORUS of peepers and crickets accompanied me as I walked across the lawn at dusk and headed west along the shore path. It was such a gorgeous night, with clear skies and a cooling breeze. I wore black pants and a halter topped with a black cardigan, and I carried sandals. I wanted to look nice for Brendan and I thought that I looked passable. I am no beauty queen, but I dress up okay.

There was a small guesthouse in a clearing by the lake with an attached bluestone patio. I saw steaks marinating and a bottle of red and Brendan stirring coals in the barbecue, raising sparks into the sky.

He kissed me, and he *was* a good kisser. His kisses lingered on the lips. "Special occasion," he said, handing me a glass of wine. "My birthday."

"Ohhh, Brendan. Jeez Louise. Why didn't you tell me?" I know that I turned the brightest shade of red, and I felt just terrible.

"I didn't want any fuss," he said, and shrugged. "It's not a big birthday. Doesn't have any zeros in it."

I did the math. He was forty-one. *Only forty-one.* I clinked my glass against his and said, "Happy, happy birthday!" I held back all the coulda-woulda stuff.

"I love it that you're here," he said. "It *is* a happy birthday."

The fireflies traced cursive neon letters in the night air as I tossed the salad and Brendan put the steaks on the grill. There was a CD player in the guesthouse, and soon Eva Cassidy was remembering the night as only she can. Brendan asked me to dance. I took his hand and immediately felt the blood rush to my head. He wrapped me in his arms and shuffled with me barefoot on the grass. Simple as this was, I loved it. Eva was followed by Sting on Brendan's personalized CD.

He was a good dancer, very coordinated, even barefoot in the grass. He could lead, or follow, and he was so light on his feet that I felt as if I were blending into him. The two of us floated over the lawn, cheek to cheek. It was so nice — glorious, actually. The two of us fit together.

"The steaks are burning," I whispered as Toni Braxton started in on "Unbreak My Heart."

"Doesn't matter," said Brendan.

"You're an incredible Prince Charming, you know. Handsome, witty, sensitive for a football fan."

He smiled at me. "What a nice birthday thought."

"After we eat," I said, "I have a really nice present for you. I've been thinking about it all afternoon."

"So you must have known it was my birthday."

"I'm improvising," I said, and smiled.

So we ate first and drank some delicious wine from somewhere in Washington State. *Two* bottles. We danced to Jill Scott and Sade and then . . . well, it *was* his birthday after all.

The guesthouse was filled with chintz-covered furniture and had a great bed looking out over the lake. That's where Brendan and I made love until "we couldn't keep our eyes open any longer." He was an incredible Prince Charming, in every way I could imagine. Even on his birthday.

I remember something else sweet. Just before we finally fell asleep, I sang, "Happy birthday, sweet Brendan. Happy birthday to you." I sang it with all my heart, and he joined in with all of his.

Forty-six

~

I AWOKE in the guesthouse with a mild headache from the wine I'd had, followed by a start of fear when I realized that I was alone. From the height of the sun, I estimated that a portion of the morning was gone as well. I gathered up my clothes and, to my relief, found a note lying on top of my sandals.

Dear Jen,

I was right, you are the best. I have a little business in Chicago. Nothing too important. See you tonight? I hope so. I can't wait to have you back in my arms. I miss you already. Hope you feel the same about moi.

    XOXO,

                        Brendan

I clutched the note to my chest as I hurried across three back lawns in last night's black clothes. Euphoria and Sox greeted me at the top of Sam's porch stairs, weaving between my legs and complaining that their breakfast was late.

As I made my apologies, a red truck pulled into the parking area. Sam's gardener spilled out of the cab. I could see that Henry was in a state. Now what?

He called out, "Jennifer, everybody has been trying to find you."

At the same moment, I could hear the telephone ringing inside. *Not Sam*, I thought.

"One minute, Henry!" I called to him. "Telephone."

I threw open the back door and fumbled with the receiver before clapping it to my

ear. I knew the caller's voice immediately —
Dr. Max — but he sounded tenuous and
strained. Not like himself.

"Sam is awake," he said. "Come right
now."

Forty-seven

~

I GUNNED the Jag up Highway 50, tapped the brakes to take a right onto 67, and sped on. All of my thoughts were on Sam, so I didn't notice that Henry was following me. Not until his pickup truck pulled alongside me in the hospital parking lot and Henry cranked down his window. "She's been —"

"Sorry, what, Henry?" I yelled back to him. "I didn't hear you!"

"Sam's not in the ICU anymore. She's on the second floor. Twenty-one B."

"Thanks!" I shouted. Then I had a thought — *Could Henry be Doc?* He had brought up two children himself. He might even have a doctorate. I thought I remembered something about that.

Then I was too busy running and semi-politely elbowing my way through the milling crowd in the hospital lobby. I took the fire stairs two at a time. I found Sam's new room at the end of a gleaming lino-leum hallway. I pushed open the swinging door. I even had a wisecrack ready: "It's about time you rejoined the living!" But I never got to say it.

My heart sank. Sam was lying absolutely still in the bed. Her eyes were closed tight. Dr. Max was bent over her, taking her vitals. *Oh God, I was too late.*

"What's happened?" I asked. "I got here as fast as I could."

Max turned and saw me. "Let's talk outside," he said. "C'mon with me."

"She's gone back into the coma, hasn't she?"

Max held up a hand to stop me from coming farther into the room. "No, Jennifer. She's out of the coma. But this is a good time for me to fill you in on some things."

We went to his office again, a beige square with prefab furnishings and inter-office memos tacked to the walls. As he'd done a couple of weeks before, Max led me to his swivel chair, then sat on the desk ledge, facing me.

"She's just sleeping," he finally said. "She was awake earlier. We tried to find you. No-body answered the phone."

"But she's out of the coma?" I asked.

"Coma is not a restful state," Max con-tinued, as if I hadn't asked him a ques-tion. "Even though they're unconscious, they still worry about stuff like who's feed-ing the dog, watering the houseplants, whether they've left the lights on. It's good for the patient to be reassured — that's why we stopped the hospital from ship-ping Sam off to St. Luke's in Milwaukee. We wanted her friends — especially you — to talk to her."

"Ship her off? This is the first I've heard."

"I know. Look" — Max waved a dismissive hand — "there was no need to get into it with you. A lot of people around here love Sam."

As I turned over that piece of news, Max explained that his father was on the hospital board. The two of them had pulled a few strings to keep Sam in Lake Geneva. Dr. Max went on to say that Lakeland Medical wasn't big enough to give patients long-term care. "Sam *is* out of her coma, but the trauma might have left her with physical or psychological difficulties."

"Did it?" I asked. "C'mon, Max, give me something here."

"She's talkative, but she doesn't always make perfect sense. She's weak. We'll keep her for a little while longer. Then she's going to need patience and a lot of care."

Max was staring at me, but why? In a flash of clarity, I realized what he was seeing. Smudged mascara under my eyes, sleep-smooshed hair — *and* I was wearing last night's rumpled clothes at 10:00 on a weekday morning.

Still, I maintained my dignity. "I want to see Sam," I told him. "Okay?"

"Absolutely. I just wanted to prepare you."

Max went with me back to Sam's room, then he left and I quietly approached her bed. I gently touched her arm. Suddenly Sam's eyelids flew open, and I jumped back. But her eyes twinkled as she looked me up and down.

"Jennifer," she said, and then smiled. "My girl is here."

Forty-eight

~

I BURST into tears and placed my arms around Sam's neck. It was so incredible, so unbelievable to feel her arms on me, to hear her voice again. I had almost given up hope that I would ever talk to her again.

She gently patted my back, just the way she'd done from the time I was two years old. I loved Sam so much that it was beyond scary to think of losing her. I'd wanted to see her again, to talk to her, and now it was happening.

I fluffed up Sam's pillow and sat on the edge of the bed. "Where have you been?" I whispered.

"I've been right here. Or so I've been told."

"Tell me," I said. It was one of our catch-phrases. *Tell me* who you're seeing in Chicago. *Tell me* the scoop at the lake.

"Well, it was . . . strange," she said, pursing her lips. "I didn't know where I was . . . but I could *hear* things, Laura."

Oops. Laura was my mother's name.

Sam continued, unaware of her mistake. "The damned *elephant* over there almost drove me mad. But when the nurses came in, they barked about the daughters. I liked that!"

I translated as best I could. The "elephant" had to be the ventilator. *Barked about the daughters?* Who knew what that was?

"Did I say *daughters?* I meant . . ."

"Doctors?" I guessed.

"Right. I knew you'd understand. I tried to talk to you, Jennifer. I could hear you, but my voice —" She pointed repeatedly, *wordlessly,* at her mouth. "Nothing came out."

I nodded, because my voice felt trapped, too. Then both of us were hugging again. When in doubt, hug. I could count her ribs through her gown, her hands shook, and her words were jumbled — but it was okay. Sam was alive. She was talking to me again. This was what I had wished and prayed for.

Sam wanted me to talk for a while, so I did, and wound up telling her more than I had planned to about Brendan and me. Sam listened, but she didn't say very much. I wondered if she was following me at all.

Then Sam looked at me with her bright blue eyes and just about broke my heart. She said, "I want to go home before I die."

Forty-nine

~

MY RELIEF at seeing and talking to Sam faded some then, and even more as I drove back to Knollwood Road later in the afternoon. I needed to call her friends, but I had begun to worry about Brendan. What was he doing in Chicago? Was his tumor getting worse? Why would he leave Lake Geneva now? Plus I couldn't wait to tell him what had happened with Sam.

I didn't like being apart from Brendan, I realized that afternoon. I hated it, actually, and that was a bad sign.

I looped the Jag around at the end of the drive and parked under the oak tree out front. In the past few minutes, my fears had condensed into a headache. It was sitting right behind my left eye.

Once I was inside the house, I gulped down two Advils. Then I walked to Shep's house to see if Brendan had returned. The house was dark, though. No one was there. *Brendan must still be in Chicago. Shoot. Where are you?* I really did miss him. And I was worried about him, too. Just general, neurotic, city-girl worry.

I trudged back to Sam's house, and I didn't know what to do with myself. Then I did. I took a packet of Sam's letters out to the porch. More than ever, I wanted to hear her stories.

What happened between her and Doc? Who was he? Would she ever tell me the whole truth? Was John Farley Doc? Was Henry? Or even Brendan's uncle Shep? Or was it someone I didn't even know?

I'd just settled into my favorite rocker when the sky darkened over the lake. The air was dense with ozone, and the imminent thunderstorm fueled a feeling of urgency about the letters. The pathetic fallacy strikes again, just like in a Brontë novel.

I *needed* to know how Sam and Doc's story turned out. I guess I wanted a happy ending. Who doesn't? But I had noticed lately that happy endings can be hard to come by.

I started to read anyway.

Fifty

∼

Jennifer dear,

The longing I felt for Doc was unbearable at times. You can imagine. Sometimes it lasted for months. Here's what happened next. There were ten days every summer that were more torturous than all the rest. It was when Charles traipsed off to Ireland to play golf with his buddies and I don't know what else they did over there, though I'd heard rumors. While he was gone, all I thought about was Doc. I couldn't help it, and maybe I didn't really want to.

I remember one particular Saturday

morning, in August of 1972. Charles was in Kilkenny and I was in downtown Lake Geneva.

All alone, as usual.

The back of my Jeepster was loaded with deer fencing when I stopped off for gas. Young Johnny Masterson was the gasoline jockey that summer, and he'd just filled up my tank when Doc's car pulled in on the other side of the pumps.

My heart started booming as soon as I saw him. This always happened, maybe partly because we had so many secrets but mostly because we were deeply in love. I gave Johnny a ten-dollar bill, and while he was getting the change, Doc stepped out of his car. He walked up to the Jeep. God, he was so handsome, Jen, with a smile that could warm anybody's heart. And those eyes of his.

"Do me a favor, Sammy," he said. "Don't fight me on this. Just follow me out of here when I leave."

529000741

I followed Doc for ten miles down Route 50, then he turned off onto the main highway. When we got to the Alpine Valley Resort, I parked my car next to his, then got into the passenger seat beside him. Was this what Doc wanted? Well, I did, too.

I went straight into his arms. "I've missed you. God, I don't know how much more of this I can stand," I confessed.

When Doc spoke, his voice made every cell in my body sing. "I know we've talked it to death, Samantha. Maybe it's wrong, but I just don't care anymore. I'm fifty years old. I love you more than I love anything in this world. I want to be alone with you. Please say you'll come away with me. *Now,* Samantha."

Jennifer, it was like exhaling after holding my breath for years. Suddenly the moment was there. All I had to do was grab it. What I'd dreamed about but hadn't dared believe could happen.

"Yes," I whispered against Doc's cheek. "I'll go away with you. Let's do it right now. Before I can even think about changing my mind."

Fifty-one

~

Jennifer,

No one else knows about this — only you.

Doc and I held each other for a long time in that parking lot. We were probably trying to keep up our nerve. I had no idea where we were going, but a few moments later we were on our way.

We held each other for the entire trip, and a hundred different, crazy thoughts were racing through my mind. What if we were caught? What would it mean to our lives? Could Doc and I make it through a whole weekend together?

We had been traveling for eight hours

when a WELCOME TO COPPER HARBOR, MICHI-
GAN sign appeared in the headlights.

"This is it," Doc said. I squeezed his
hand tightly, then scooched up and kissed
him. *This was it, all right*. For the record,
Copper Harbor is at the tip of Michigan's
Keweenaw Peninsula, surrounded on
three sides by Lake Superior. It's a stagger-
ingly beautiful place. The air was cool in
August, and I was wearing only shorts and
a sleeveless shirt. Doc took off his jacket
and draped it around my shoulders.

"It's called Raptor Lodge, and it's very
small, very special," he told me. "I've
wanted to bring you here for a long time."

I laughed. "And I've wanted to come
with you, anywhere at all. But *this* is
beautiful."

We walked into the main building and
registered. I'm certain that we looked very
much in love, and, Jennifer, we were. I gen-
erally don't like couples who are all over
each other, but I couldn't help myself, and
neither could Doc.

   We walked to our room from the main lodge, and I couldn't let go of him. The night was alive with hoots and whistles and a light crackle as animals stepped through the underbrush. Nothing mattered to me but Doc and being close to him and what was going to happen next. In my whole life, I had been with only Charles, and look how that had worked out.

   We finally saw our cabin in a moonlit clearing carpeted with pine needles. My mouth was suddenly dry as Doc fumbled with the key. My legs were shaking, too. Then he swung open the door and pulled me into his arms.

   "Finally," Doc said, and smiled.

   We kissed and started to pull at each other's clothes. Doc was kissing and touching me in ways I'd never experienced before. If this bothers you, go to the next letter, but it was so good for me. I was melting in his arms, and all my doubts about myself were dissolving, too. I felt sexy and wanted, beautiful, and even pretty good in bed. I had never known it could be like that, because it had never been even close to that good for me. I felt alive and free and *desirable*. I felt like a woman, and I loved every second of it.

Finally, Doc cupped my face in his hands and stared deeply into my eyes.

"You have *no* idea how beautiful you are, do you?" he asked, and seemed amazed at my naïveté.

"No," I told him, "no idea at all. Not until I met you."

Fifty-two

~

Jennifer,

I do have a few juicy details that I won't
share with you, but that night with Doc
was everything I had wanted it to be and
so much more. I woke up in his arms and
for the first time I could remember, I felt I
was where I belonged. "Morning, Samantha," he whispered. "You're still as beautiful as I remember from last night."

I was *Samantha* to Doc — only to him.

We stayed in our cabin for most of the
next two days. The truth is, we didn't want
to be anywhere else. Everything was so
new for us, and the exploration was, well,

so much fun. On the second night, a ring-ing telephone jarred us awake.

I held on to Doc's arm and I started to shake a little. No one knew we were there. Had Charles found us?

"Very good. Thanks," Doc spoke into the receiver. Now I was even more mystified. I didn't understand why he was smiling about being woken up from a sound sleep at quarter to two.

"Get dressed, Samantha," he said, grab-bing for his clothes. "You're going to like this. It's part of the reason we're here."

Jennifer, imagine this. Just try to imagine what we did that night.

We took a short ride in the car, then walked, and ended up sitting on a huge boulder looking out over Lake Superior. I was hugging my knees. Doc had an arm around me, and the *only* thing between us and Canada was the vast glassy expanse of the lake. It was a little before three in the morning.

As we watched, as our eyes went wide, a glowing ribbon of green light stretched across the horizon and then drifted lazily upward, until it became a transparent curtain shimmering above the water. The hem of the curtain brightened with a reddish gleam, then veils of purple and blue flared, and the sky seemed to shiver and sway.

"Someone spiked the water," I managed to gasp. "Or I'm hallucinating."

Doc laughed. "This is the aurora borealis. Most people know the name, but they have no idea what it is. Now we do, Samantha. Isn't this amazing?"

It was an unforgettable moment. The entire sky was in motion, and as the undulating curtain passed right over us, bright points of light swirled like pinwheels. Doc said that the aurora was actually a stream of electrons powered by the solar wind, colliding with atoms of gas. "The impact causes the gas to emit light. The color of the light depends on the type of gas. The green and red lights are oxygen, blue and purple are hydrogen and helium. Sodium is yellow. It's like neon lighting without the tubes," Doc said. "It's neon in the wild."

I hugged him and whispered, "Thank you for this."

Doc shrugged. "I just arranged for us to be awake to see it."

"Don't let this end," I whispered against his cheek. And it didn't. Doc and I made love that night on a boulder under starry skies. Jennifer, it was an out-of-body, out-of-this-world experience, and I highly recommend "neon in the wild" to anybody with a little romance left in their souls.

Even if they're not quite sure if it's still there.

Fifty-three

Dear Jen,

Sunday morning came, and I woke up feeling sad and afraid. I wanted to leave Charles. Studying his face, I watched Doc sleep, his full head of blond hair, just lightly touched with silver. I memorized everything about how Doc looked, hating that it had to come to this. Time to collect my memories.

"I'm awake," he whispered. "I was just thinking with my eyes shut."

"About?"

"Oh, everything we did this weekend. You. You're even better than the aurora borealis."

I didn't complain — not a word, not a look. But Doc knew. "Don't be sad, Samantha," he said. "We just had the best weekend ever."

"I want to be with you," I told him. "I don't want us to be apart anymore. I don't think I can stand it."

"You read my mind," Doc said. "But I've been thinking about that for *years*. This divided life of ours, it can be, well, heartbreaking as hell. When Sara was sick, when we knew for sure that she was dying, I promised that I would raise our boys in a way she would always approve of. And you, you'd have to divorce Charles, and he'd fight it, wouldn't he?"

I put a finger to Doc's lips, not because I didn't want to hear what he had to say but because I could see the pain that it was causing him.

"When you're ready," I said, "I'll be waiting for you. There's one more thing that has to be said, so I'll say it. I love you so much. I feel like you saved my life."

"I love you, Samantha."

God, I loved hearing those words.

I was in a kind of daze as we said good-bye to the inn's owners, Mr. and Mrs. Lundstrom, and the hazy feeling continued for much of the drive back to Lake Geneva. I remember holding Doc's hand the whole way.

Then we were pulling into the parking lot of the Alpine Valley Resort. What an incredible letdown that was, what a heartbreaking moment. We held each other for a long time, just held on for dear life in Doc's car.

"I have to go, Samantha," he finally said.

"I miss you already, and you're not even gone," I whispered. "Please miss me, too."

"What a beautiful thing to say," Doc told me. "I love your humility." Then we kissed one last time, and I hoped it *wasn't* for the last time. It took all my willpower and strength not to bawl like a baby in his arms. But I *didn't* cry.

My Jeep was where I had left it. I got inside, and everything seemed unreal to my touch. We honked our farewells, and I pulled out onto the highway. I let him speed ahead.

As I made my way back to Lake Geneva alone, I thought about the aurora borealis, but also about losing Doc, and how I could possibly bear it. I cried all the way home.

Fifty-four

~

POOR SAM.

A wind-driven rain forced me off the porch and into the darkening house. Sam's loneliness, the unexpected sadness in her life, clung to me as I closed windows and mopped up raindrops from the window-sills. I thought about her good-bye to Doc, which sent my thoughts to Brendan. *Where is he? It's just awful outside. Teeming rain, and he's driving in it.*

I put Sam's remaining letters on the mantel next to the old marble clock — and that's when something else hit me. I had a deadline at 6:00 P.M. I'd completely forgotten about my column.

214

I settled into the blue velvet embrace of the sofa, booted up my laptop, and called up my file of rainy-day notions. Not one of them was worthy of 750 words, but after a couple of hours, a big idea did float up from the deep well of my brain.

It was so big, in fact, I wondered why it had taken me so long to come up with it.

I picked up the phone and punched in a number that I knew by heart.

"Debbie, there's no getting around this," I said. "I'm no good to the *Trib* right now, and I'm not being fair to my readers. It's hard to explain. So hard, I won't even try."

I told my editor how sorry I was, but I had to take a leave of absence. But I didn't tell her why. I didn't want Debbie's sympathy, and I didn't want to have to explain myself and what was going on with Sam and with Brendan.

When I clicked off the phone, I felt a rush of anxiety. It was like standing on the edge of a cliff and staring down into darkness and nothingness.

I still needed to visit Sam that night, but the rain was absolutely sheeting outside, obscuring the lake, even the trees beside the house. I almost made it out to the Jag when the single toot of a car horn got my attention. *Brendan!* He was driving his black Jeep down the puddle-soaked lane behind the houses.

He rolled down the side window and smiled, and all was forgiven. "Jenniferrrrr. I'm back. The rain was terrible all the way from Chicago."

I was soooo glad to see Brendan's smiling face. *There's your explanation, Debbie! That smile of his.* I tacked to the left and leaned a dripping, yellow-slickered elbow into the open window.

"Hey, buddy, mind if I hop in with you? I have news. Sam is out of her coma."

Fifty-five

~

"YOU'RE GOING to love her. Sam's much more interesting when she's conscious," I told Brendan as we rode to the hospital. "And she's going to like you, I guess. Or she'll pretend to, anyway."

Brendan started to laugh. "What's gotten into you?" he asked.

"Oh, I just heard a sad story, and then I saw your smiling face. Strange, interesting juxtaposition. I also took a leave of absence at work. Now I'm a beach bum, just like you." Brendan and I slapped high-fives over that one.

We arrived at Sam's room, and — what was this? — dozens of shiny Mylar balloons

217

and streamers hung from the ceiling, with cellophane-wrapped baskets of fruit and gaudy flower arrangements competing for space on the counters and tables. Obviously, word had gotten around Lake Geneva, and maybe the rest of Wisconsin and Illinois, that Sam was conscious. I wondered if any of the flowers or balloons were from Doc.

She was wearing a blue-striped hospital gown and her complexion was still gray, but her hair was combed and she smiled when she saw me. She was alert and seemed almost herself.

"Hello. Hello, Jennifer. And who's the handsome one?" she asked.

"This is Brendan. I told you about him, but you probably don't remember. He is kind of handsome, isn't he?"

Brendan reached out and shook her hand. "Hiya, Samantha," he said, and my jaw dropped. I had no idea where that came from. *Samantha?* Like in the letters. That was what Doc always called her.

"Don't I know you?" Sam said. "You look like — oh, you know who."

"My uncle Shep?" asked Brendan. "Just a wild guess."

"That's the one," she said. "Of course you do."

Brendan cranked up Sam's bed a couple of notches; then we pulled a couple of chairs close. Sam started to give us a slightly fractured discourse on her day. But then she turned her eyes back to Brendan. She seemed just a little confused again. "I'm fine," she said, and winked at me.

Then she looked at Brendan again. "I hear you're a very good doctor, Brendan. So why have you given up hope?" Sam asked. "How can you leave somebody as special as Jennifer without a fight?"

I saw Brendan's head go back as if he'd taken a punch in the nose, but then he recovered nicely. "It's a good question, isn't it? It's the one I've been asking myself."

My eyes connected with Sam's. I don't

know how, but she had gone right to the heart of the matter. *Wham, bam, thank you, Sam.*

"As you said, Samantha, I'm a doctor. We're a logical bunch, for the most part. Maybe too logical for our own good sometimes. I want to enjoy whatever time I have left, whatever time *we* have left, okay? I don't want to waste a second of it. Not one second. Does that make sense to you?"

Sam stared into his eyes and nodded. "Seems like a pretty reasonable philosophy," she said. "Hard to argue with."

"Thank you," Brendan said.

"So?" Sam said, her eyes going to me, then back to Brendan.

"So?" I said. Brave smile.

Sam's eyes stayed on Brendan now. "Fight it," she whispered. "I did."

Fifty-six

~

THE NEXT FEW DAYS were possibly the best, and most memorable, of my life. I was trying to live every day from sunup until I couldn't keep my eyes open. Suddenly it made all the sense in the world to me. I had a lot of time to make up with both Sam and Brendan.

Brendan was a reflective person who liked to think things through, but he also loved to top off his best thoughts by saying something funny, usually at his own expense, which fit with the way I saw the world. I was discovering that he had the most generous and giving nature. He wasn't overly protective, but he was there for me when I needed him.

Every time I looked into his eyes, or even saw him at a distance, I couldn't help thinking what a senseless, awful, messed-up waste it was that he was going to die. I wanted to argue with him about his decision, but I just couldn't fight. He was too smart, too nice; besides, it would have been a waste of our time together. The precious seconds of our summer.

We went swimming every day, even in the rain. We visited Sam, sometimes three times a day, and she and Brendan became friends. They were actually a lot alike. Brendan and I took long walks, and we had dinner together every night. We didn't eat much during the day, but dinner was always special.

Except for those blueberry pancakes, Brendan was *not* a good cook — though given more time to practice, he swore that he could be mediocre. So I cooked the meals; he did setup and cleanup. When he worked, he wore this Red Cross lifeguard T-shirt that I loved on him.

We really liked to dance to a favorite CD, or just the radio. I loved to be held by him, to be close, to listen to Brendan hum along to a song like "Something to Talk About." Or Jill Scott's "Do You Remember," or "Sweet Baby James," "The Logical Song," "Bad to the Bone," "Let's Spend the Night Together." Dozens of others, rockers and ballads — it didn't much matter.

They were our songs, the songs of our summer.

One Sunday night Brendan fell asleep before I did, so I took one of the last packets of Sam's letters into the kitchen. I had counted the letters recently — there were 170 of them. The longest was nearly twenty pages; the shortest, just a paragraph. I'd gone through at least three-quarters of them. Sam's legacy to me. I'd be finished with her letters soon.

I sat at the kitchen table under the harsh glare of an overhead light, and I read my grandmother's next entry.

Dear Jennifer,

After Doc and I returned from Copper Harbor, our separation was even worse than I had thought it would be. *Much worse.* Which meant that we were deeply in love, terribly in love. But this I already knew. During a late-night phone call that fall, we arrived at the inevitable conclusion: we had to be together again.

But then we had to wait months, and when Charles planned another golfing (or whatever) trip in June, I made plans, too. I also picked our destination: the town of Holland on the eastern shore of Lake Michigan.

As we'd done before, Doc and I met in the parking lot at Alpine Valley. We hugged and kissed and grinned like teenagers watching the submarine races. Then we took to the road. It was a six-hour journey:

a two-hour drive followed by four hours on the S.S. *Badger,* a car ferry that was a minivacation in itself.

I never wanted to leave Doc again. The two of us leaned over the railing and watched the ferry's engines distance us from our real lives with miles of churning wake. We had hot chocolate at the restaurant onboard and saw our first movie together (*The Pink Panther*) in the *Badger*'s tiny theater. By the time we reached shore, our skin was flushed and our hearts were singing. We were so much in love, and our weekend in Michigan was even better than the first. Neil Simon hadn't written *Same Time, Next Year* yet, but Doc and I were living it anyway.

Jennifer, I'm going to shorthand this just a little and stick to the high points, and the low ones.

The next summer Charles took his trip in July, and again Doc and I made our plans around his departure. We drove north, but then Doc surprised me. He had rented a houseboat in La Crosse, Wisconsin, a place where three rivers converge: the La Crosse, the Black, and the Mississippi. We set our course, and an hour and a half later we docked in the small town of Wabasha, Minnesota. Doc and I celebrated with roast pheasant, baked raisin beans, squash rolls, and apple brandy pie. Possibly the best meal ever. Afterward, we motored back down to the marina in La Crosse and anchored for the night. We stayed in a double berth under the sundeck. The next morning we showered on the deck, squealing under the spray. Then we joined a flotilla of every kind of craft imaginable in the annual Riverfest. There were late-night bands on the water, fireworks, and happy children everywhere. Especially Doc and me. For four days I was in heaven, and I didn't want to return to earth. But, of course, I had to.

The plan for our fourth annual was a glamorous trip to New York City, which I looked forward to for a full nine months.

We booked a room at the Plaza overlooking Central Park, had tickets for two Broadway plays, box seats at Yankee Stadium, restaurant reservations. This would be our best time together yet.

As we waited in the flight lounge at O'Hare, clients of Charles's who were booked on the same flight to New York saw me and called my name. I nearly fainted and turned the brightest shade of red.

Doc was leafing through the *New York Times* just a few yards away when he saw me greet the Hennesseys and make up a story about seeing a friend off on another flight. Doc got the picture and slipped away. As soon as we could, we met up again. We decided against New York and headed to his car. My heart was broken in little pieces.

"A fine kettle of fish you've gotten us into this time, Stanley," Doc said. He switched on the car's ignition.

"I just lied to the Hennesseys," I said.

227

"They're going to tell Charles. We should head right home."

Doc nodded sadly, backed out of the parking space, then drove from the airport. It was such a beautiful morning, so bright with promise. What a shame. My mind whirred with heartbreaking disappointment as we eased into the stream of traffic on the exit ramp.

"You know," I said, "I have another idea."

Doc smiled ear to ear. "I knew you would, Samantha. No way I was going to take you home, anyway."

Fifty-seven

~

Jennifer,

The Lundstroms were obviously surprised when we arrived at the door of the
lodge at nightfall, but they were also glad
to see us and they had room. Once we had
a key, Doc and I headed up the familiar
moonlit trail that was alive with the sounds
of the woods. I couldn't wait to be in Doc's
arms again. We'd already wasted half a day.

I'll remember this for the rest of my life.
Just when we rounded a bend in the path,
a shadow crashed out of the underbrush
and into the pathway. I didn't know what
it was, but it was bigger than a horse and
smelled horribly. The thing brayed at us! I

guess we gave it a scare, too. Doc and I froze as the beast clattered across the trail and down the hillside.

"That was a moose," Doc said, finally picking up our suitcases and the flashlight. We hurried to the cabin. Of course we couldn't sleep. And late on the Night of the Moose, we finally laughed about our close call at O'Hare. Then we made a plan to make sure it didn't happen again. From that day on, we spent our lost weekends on Michigan's Upper Peninsula. Mike and Marge Lundstrom became our good friends, and the cabin in Copper Harbor, with its fieldstone fireplace in the bedroom and view of Lake Superior, became our hideaway.

No one back home ever knew our secret, Jennifer. No one guessed about Doc and me, and our double life.

And don't you dare tell.

Don't put it in any of your columns, either.

Or, God forbid, a book.

Fifty-eight

~

Dear Jen,

This happened four years ago, but I couldn't tell you how I really felt about it. Not until now.

It was a chilly March night and snow was falling softly in Chicago, a great deal of snow. The wind was howling like a wounded animal, of course. Your grandfather and I were about to get ready for bed when he asked me to go out for a bottle of anisette. He had indigestion and thought the liquor would settle his stomach. It had worked before.

I had always taken care of Charles's needs and cared for him as much as I could, given how he had treated me. I had to go quickly because the package store would be closing soon. So out I went into the snow and wind. "Sam the dependable one" Charles called me sometimes, always thinking he was being endearing rather than condescending.

When I came back twenty minutes later, your grandfather was dead in his bed.

Jen, he looked just as when I had left him; wearing his favorite blue pj's from Henri Bendel, a Macanudo still burning in the ashtray, and the television tuned to the nightly news. It still shocks me when I think about how quickly he was gone. The heart attack must have come on him like a blown-out tire that slams a car into a telephone pole. Total devastation in an instant.

None of us even knew that his heart was bad. But Charles had never been careful about what he ate or drank or smoked, or especially how he carried on late at night. Jennifer, despite all the things

I've told you in these letters, we had children and grandchildren and many, many shared experiences. When I looked at him in repose, I saw the face of the young man I had known many years before. A quick-witted boy who'd fought in a war, been unloved by his parents, and had struggled greatly to make his place in the world. I remembered the promise I'd felt for us in those early days, the love I'd wanted to give Charles, and certainly would have.

So sad. But some stories simply are.

Fifty-nine

~

THE NEXT MORNING I had a long, emotional talk with Sam about my grandfather, and about Doc. It was the best talk we'd had since she came out of the coma, and she was seeming more like herself every day.

"I read some more of the letters last night," I told her soon after I arrived. "I'm doing it the way you asked, a few at a time. I read about Grandpa Charles dying last night. It made me cry, Sam. Did you cry? You didn't say in the letter."

Sam took my hand. "Oh, of course I did. I could have had so much love in my heart for Charles, but he just wouldn't let me

234

give it to him. He was a smart man in many ways, but so stubborn in others. I think he was so hurt by his father and his uncle that he never trusted anyone again. I really don't know, Jennifer. You see, Charles wouldn't tell me *his* story."

My eyes welled up with tears. All of this was so sad to hear. "He was always good to me, Sam."

"I know that, Jennifer. I know he was."

"He did have a temper, and there were always Grandpa Charles's rules of behavior in Chicago, and even here at the lake."

Sam finally smiled. "Oh, you don't have to tell me about Charles's rules of proper behavior. I know them by heart. And all about his temper, too."

I looked into her eyes, trying to understand everything. "So why didn't you leave him?"

Sam just smiled. "Finish the letters and we'll talk more. Just remember, they're not only about me — the letters are about you, too, sweetheart."

I had to laugh. "Sam's rules, huh?"

"Not rules, Jennifer. Just a different road I traveled. Just my side of things."

"And you're not going to tell me who Doc is, are you?"

"I'm not going to tell you, Jennifer. Read the letters. Maybe you'll be able to guess."

Sixty

~

BRENDAN AND I got a swim in just about every night at twilight. That evening I appeared in a blue Speedo racing suit with red piping, looking every inch the Big Ten swim champion that I wasn't. Brendan had on a pair of black boxers that weren't too boxy and fit him just right.

"You look really good," I told him. "Is that a sexist thing to say? Hey, who cares?"

"*You* look beautiful," Brendan said. Then his face turned unusually serious. "You're a gorgeous woman, Jennifer."

I hadn't heard compliments like those for a while, and I was starting to half believe them. I certainly liked hearing nice things about myself. Who doesn't? Maybe Cameron Diaz is sick of hearing compliments, but not me.

"Just stunning, Jen. You could have been in the movies," he continued.

"Don't blow it," I told him. "You should probably stop right there."

"Sorry, it's just the way I feel. One man's opinion. Others might look at you and see, oh, I don't know, Rosie —"

"You *are* going to blow it."

"But I see the most beautiful girl in the world."

I shook my head. "No, Brendan. Too over the top. Pull it back some. Not *too* far back."

"How about on the lake? Most beautiful on the lake?"

I shrugged, grinned. "*Maybe*. At this moment on the lake, which is mostly deserted."

"Well, that's settled — most beautiful girl on the lake!"

And then Brendan let go with maybe his loudest banshee scream yet. He almost sounded in pain. He took off for the water a step ahead of me.

But just a step.

"Last one to the buoy!" he turned and yelled.

"Last one to the buoy — what?"

"Is the biggest *loser* in the world!"

"Too much of an overstatement."

"Biggest loser on Lake Geneva! That we can see in our line of vision at this moment!"

"You're on!"

We hit the water and began to stroke furiously. I was feeling good and thought I wouldn't lose by as wide a margin as usual, which I, of course, would consider a huge victory. Moments later I reached out of the water for the buoy. To my surprise, Brendan grabbed the bobbing marker a couple of seconds behind me. I shook water off my face and hair.

"No fair! You *let* me win!" I yelped.

Brendan stared into my eyes. He was smiling, but there was something else in those eyes.

"No, Jennifer, I didn't."

Sixty-one

~

IT RAINED like the dickens the next day, and Brendan disappeared for several hours. He was starting to worry me, I'll admit. I was afraid that he might not come back one of these times, that he could get terribly sick or black out while driving, something bad. The rain had slowed to a light drizzle by the time he pulled into the driveway about four.

I couldn't wait to see him, so I ran outside into the rain and kissed him through the open window. I was so *happy* to see Brendan.

"Where'd you go?" I asked. "I woke up about seven and you were gone."

"Had a doctor's appointment in Chicago. You were snoring your pretty head off. I thought I'd let you sleep."

I made a face. "*I* don't snore."

"No, of course not." Then Brendan shot me one of his grins.

I didn't completely let him off the hook. "What did the doctor say?"

Brendan blinked, evidently composing what he was about to tell me. "The tumor is getting bigger," he said at last. "Not the greatest news, I'm afraid. Not too much of a surprise, though."

Then he covered the left side of his face with his hand. He drummed his fingers on his cheekbone. "I'm losing some mobility, Jennifer. Face is getting numb. I can't feel *this*."

I stroked his cheekbone myself.

"Sorry. I can't feel that, either. But I love your touch anyway. I love everything about you, Jennifer. Don't you forget that."

Brendan struggled with his footing when

getting out of his Jeep. He almost fell. I was stunned, and suddenly realized how bad his day must have been. He smiled, though, and then touched my cheek. "I need a little nap. I think I'll go over to Shep's. I'll see you later, Jen."

"Are you okay?" I asked. I wanted to take Brendan's arm, to help him, but I was afraid he might not like it.

"Sure I am. Just tired. I'm fine. Just need a nap."

It was only four in the afternoon, but I lay down with Brendan anyway. I wanted to be beside him, to feel his touch, to let him know that I was there for him. I was petrified inside, maybe realizing for the first time that I *was* going to lose Brendan and feeling what it would be like, and hating the feeling so much.

"Thanks," he whispered. "Tired."

Then he was gone.

Brendan slept in spurts. He clenched his fists several times. After about fifteen minutes, his eyes snapped open and he looked dazed. "Oh boy, Jennifer. Seems I dozed off, huh? More like I fell off a cliff."

I asked if he was in any pain and he answered by asking me to get a bottle of pills from his jacket. When I returned, his bed was empty and I heard him being sick in the bathroom. I was starting to get really scared now. I wasn't ready for this. Brendan had told me repeatedly that he could get worse in a hurry, but I'd chosen not to believe it.

"Jen, the Percocet is going to knock me out," he said when he appeared from the bathroom. "I'll sleep right through. Why don't you go home. Please. Do it for me. I love you dearly. And you are the most beautiful girl in the world, not just the lake. Go home for a while."

This was a little strange, but I couldn't — or wouldn't — argue with him. I kissed Brendan on the forehead, on the cheek, then lightly on the lips.

"I felt that." He smiled.

So I kissed Brendan again.

And again.

The truth was, I didn't want to stop kissing him ever.

Sixty-two

I HAD a really bad feeling all through the night. Shep was at his house back in Chicago, so I checked on Brendan every couple of hours. Then I finally fell asleep back at Sam's. He'd made it clear he didn't want me with him that night. I felt I needed to respect that.

When I woke up, it was morning and I was alone in my old room. The sun burned through the gauzy curtains, and my thoughts immediately went to Brendan. And what I thought was, *Brendan is going to die soon.* And there was nothing I could do about it.

I listened for his yell — and then I remembered. I'd left him at Shep's house, knocked out by painkillers. I pulled myself out of bed and dressed in the first clean things I could find: washer-wrinkled khakis and a white T-shirt. I jammed my sockless feet into sneakers and went downstairs to the kitchen.

I looked out the window. No naked screaming men.

The Jeep was glistening in the driveway. Okay, Brendan was there. Maybe I could make him breakfast at least. I started over to Shep's.

I entered the house through the un-locked back door, called Brendan's name as I frisked the downstairs rooms with my eyes. When I didn't see any sign of him, I hurried up to his bedroom at the back of the house. The room was empty. The bed had been made with a nice white cotton spread.

It took me a moment to catch up. Brendan wasn't in the house. His things weren't there, either.

I threw open the screen door that led to the upper deck Brendan had so recently stained and waterproofed. From high up there, I scanned the yard and beyond. Brendan was nowhere to be seen.

Panic raced through me, and I tried to tamp it down. Maybe Shep would know where Brendan was. I raced back downstairs, my sneakers scuffing the polished hardwood, my eyes darting everywhere as I looked for the kitchen phone.

That's when I saw a pile of clues — obviously left for me. They were clustered on the white-laminate kitchen counter. Three items were clumped together; a white no. 10 envelope, a set of car keys, a business card with a red bird on it.

The business card was from Cardinal Transport, a local taxi service.

The keys belonged to the Jeep.

The envelope was addressed to me. When I took the envelope in my hands, I felt something loose and jiggly inside. I ripped open one end, and Brendan's watch poured out into my palm. My heart was in my throat.

There was also a letter.

Sixty-three

Dear Jennifer,

It's just after five in the morning and I'm waiting for the taxi to take me to the airport. You know, it's lonelier than you could ever imagine. I know you're going to be hurt because I'm saying good-bye like this but, please, hear me out before you make a final judgment. I'm writing while I still can. There are things I want to tell you while I can say them. I want to minimize the hurt to you if I can. I believe this is the best way, the only way for me.

Do you remember when we were kids, how we lived for summer? I'd start to get a sense of expectation in early May that the days were getting longer and I would hope that this summer the sun would keep soaring in the sky and break through to the other side. That it would be like it is in the northern regions, daylight all summer long. Then June would come and the days really were longer. But after the Fourth of July, darkness reasserted itself and we had to accept the duality of light and dark.

In the same way, Jennifer, I'd hoped, and prayed, that we'd have more time to do all the things we wanted to do together. I wanted an endless summer with you. But then darkness always comes, doesn't it? Just a fact of life, I guess.

If I know anything, it's this: Our being together was the best possible thing that could have happened, and I want to leave that feeling of rightness intact and beautiful. I love you so much. I adore you, Jennifer. I mean it. You *inspire* me. I hope with all my heart that you'll forgive me for this and that you'll understand how unbearably hard it is for me to leave you this morning. Without our swim. Or some five-star blueberry pancakes. This is the hardest thing I've ever done in my life! But I believe in my heart it's the right thing to do.

I love you so much that it hurts me to even have the thought. Please believe that.

You are my light, you are my endless summer.

Brendan

PART THREE

Leaving Lake Geneva

Sixty-four

～

BY THE TIME I'd finished reading Brendan's letter, I could barely breathe and the tears were just streaming down my face. I couldn't help thinking that somehow it was my fault he'd left. Just as it was my fault that Daniel was alone when he died in Hawaii. I slid his watch onto my wrist. Then I called Shep's law office in Chicago. I told his assistant that I had to speak with him. Finally I heard Shep's familiar, soothing voice over the phone.

"Shep, Brendan's gone," I managed to say.

"I know, Jen. I spoke with him this morning. It's for the best."

"No, it isn't," I said. "Please tell me what's going on. What is he doing?"

Shep hemmed and hawed, then told me some of the same things that Brendan had said in his letter. That he didn't want me to have to go through the final stage of his disease. That he loved me and was sick that he had to leave. And that Brendan was scared.

"I have to see him," I told Shep. "It can't end like this. I won't let it. Shep, I'll come to your office in Chicago if I have to."

I could hear Shep sigh deeply. "I think I know how you feel, but Brendan made me promise not to tell you. I gave him my word."

"Shep, I need to see him again. Don't I have anything to say about this? It's wrong to have Brendan make this decision without me."

There was a silence on the line and I was afraid Shep would hang up on me. Finally he spoke. "I promised him. You're putting me in an untenable position. Oh hell, Jennifer . . . He's on his way to the Mayo Clinic."

I couldn't believe what I'd heard. "What did you say? He's going to the hospital?"

"Mayo's the best place for this," Shep told me. "He's having experimental surgery in the morning."

Sixty-five

~

MY STOMACH was heaving, just as it had been a year and a half ago when I went to the hospital in Oahu to see Danny's body. Only now I was in my car, shifting gears literally and figuratively as I sped south on I-94 until the road split. Then I took I-294 toward O'Hare.

I called Sam on my cell, explaining what I could, and she told me I was the best fighter she knew and said she was proud of me. Then the two of us were crying over the phone, just like old times.

I'm sure people were staring at me as I boarded the American flight to Rochester, Minnesota. I was stiff-faced and distracted, and my eyes were swollen and very, very red.

A little over an hour and a half later, I drove a rented car toward the Mayo Clinic. I was going to see Brendan, I hoped, and he was just where I wanted him: at one of the best cancer hospitals in the world.

Sixty-six

~

A REVOLVING glass door deposited me into the cool green lobby of the main building of St. Marys at the Mayo Clinic, a vast space with high marble walls and free-standing columns. This was where Brendan was to be operated on. I walked to the admissions desk, explained who I was, and asked how to find his room.

I was told that "Dr. Keller preregistered earlier today. He'll be checking into the Joseph Building at six o'clock tomorrow morning. He isn't here."

The crushing disappointment must have showed on my face because the twenty-something woman at reception opened a three-ring binder. She ran a finger down a list, then looked up at me.

"He said there was a possibility someone might come."

I didn't know what to say. "Well, I did. I'm here."

"Dr. Keller is staying at the Colonial Inn, one-fourteen Second Street, Southwest," she said.

I got directions, and soon the rented car and I were back on the road. The minutes whizzed by even as rush-hour traffic pinned me in place. Finally I broke through the logjam, which I wouldn't have expected in Rochester. A few minutes later I was at the Colonial Inn, and I was shaking like a leaf.

I found room 143 and knocked. There was no response from inside.

"Brendan, please," I said. "I came all this way. It's Jennifer . . . the prettiest girl at Lake Geneva?"

The door opened slowly and Brendan was standing there, all six foot one of him. His shoulders were still broad and he looked solid. His eyes were as blue as the northern sky on a day in July. He opened his arms and took me into them.

"Hey there, Scout," he whispered. "Prettiest girl in Rochester, Minnesota."

Sixty-seven

～

"I WAS MAD at you," I finally admitted as I held Brendan tightly.

"And now? What are you feeling now, Jennifer?"

"You're charming me out of it."

"I didn't realize I was being charming," he said.

"I know. It's just part of your personality. It's something in your blue eyes."

We swayed together in the doorway for a moment or two, then broke apart. It was only now that Brendan's eyelids drooped and his movements became noticeably slower and a little shaky — from pain medication or from the tumor? We sat down on

263

the couch and I tousled the wave in his hair.

"Happy now?" he asked.

"Yep," I answered.

"God, I missed you," he said, and we kissed.

Then Brendan leaned back and stared at the ceiling. He seemed far away. "Want to hear the schedule?" he asked.

I nodded. I guess this meant that Brendan knew I wasn't going away.

He rested his hand on my knee. "Have to be at the hospital at six. Sharp. Adam Kolski is doing the surgery at seven. He's pretty good."

"Pretty good?"

"He's *really* good. Practically a godddddd," Brendan said. And suddenly there was that magnificent smile of his. "Of course I got the best."

"That's more like it," I said. And there, finally, was that smile of *mine*.

"I should warn you, after tomorrow I'm going to look like a cannon shot me head-first into a brick wall. If things go well. I hope you really do love my charm, that certain something in my eyes."

"I love everything about you," I said. "I especially love that you're going to do this."

Brendan kissed me again, and I melted. Then he said, "Let's get out of here. Let me show you Rochester. And yes, this *is* a date."

Sixty-eight

~

A DATE. That was another cute line, and it reminded me of everything that was so good about Brendan and me. We had the same energy, the same passion about a lot of things, common interests; we shared a goofy sense of humor; and it was so hard to find someone who was right for you. God, sometimes it could seem impossible. For some people it *is* impossible.

I drove and Brendan gave directions. About three or four miles from the hotel, back near the hospital, he told me to park anywhere I could find a spot. Actually, the side street we were on was surprisingly crowded for a work night.

"What's here, anyway?" I asked.

"Stephen Dunbar's Pub," Brendan said. "This is where we used to blow off steam when I was a resident. It's where I want to take you for our date."

"A bar?" I asked him. "Stephen Dunbar's Pub?"

He nodded. "I don't think I should drink tonight," Brendan said. "But I definitely think I should *dance*."

Inside, the bar was about half full, a nice, comfortable crowd, and there were couples dancing to a Red Hot Chili Peppers ballad I liked, "Under the Bridge."

Brendan immediately took me in his arms. "I like this song," he whispered against my cheek. And then we were dancing. "And I love dancing with you.

"Thank you for Jennifer," he continued to whisper. "She's the perfect one. All that I ever wanted out of life."

It sounded like a prayer to me. "I saw you praying once. In the kitchen," I confessed.

"Same exact prayer," Brendan said, and

winked at me. "I've been saying it all summer."

We danced to all the slow songs that played on the juke, and we danced slow to some of the fast ones. I didn't ever want to let Brendan go, not even for a minute.

"What could be better than this?" he asked. "A date with my best girl, in my old school town, at one of the old haunts."

I felt so incredibly close to Brendan, so much in love with him, which made what was going to happen in the morning unthinkable. I didn't want it to happen, but tears welled up in my eyes. "Stop being so sweet," I told Brendan.

"No tears," he said, and wiped them away. "No tangles," he laughed, then winced a little at his own joke. Brendan could always laugh. At any time. About anything, even this.

We continued to dance, to an old Smokey Robinson and the Miracles song. "After this is all behind us," he said, "let's travel. I've never been to Florence, or Venice. China,

Africa — there's so much to see out there, Jen."

I started to tear up again. "I can't help it. I'm not usually so sentimental," I said.

"Oh, it's kind of a sentimental time. Kiss me again. Keep kissing me. Right up until they operate."

So we kissed again. But finally we headed back to the Colonial Inn, where I thought Brendan would collapse into sleep. But he didn't.

"Every day from the crack of dawn," he said — and I completed the rest, "until we can't keep our eyes open one second longer."

About three, we finally did fall asleep in each other's arms, our fingers entwined, my head on his chest. I remember thinking, *This is the way it should be. Just like this. For many, many years.*

And then the alarm clock began to ring.

Sixty-nine

~

BRENDAN LEANED down close and gave me a kiss on the lips. He was already up and dressed. "Crack of dawn," he said. "Ready for a swim in the lake?"

"Don't make jokes now, not even good ones. Okay, Brendan?"

"My chances of surviving three years with GBM is less than —"

I cut him off. "All right, jokes are okay. Jokes are good." I came across the bed and kissed him. "I love you."

"I love you, too. Probably from the first time I ever saw you at the lake. You were, and still are, the most beautiful girl in the world. *In the world.* Got it?"

"I got it." I smiled. "Of course, it's only your opinion."

"Good point. But I happen to be right on this one."

I was pretty sure that I had my emotions under control for the moment. That's why I wasn't prepared for something so small to tear me apart. I noticed Brendan's hands shaking badly as he bent to secure a new pair of shoes that looked like his Nike cross-trainers but weren't. Instead of laces, the shoes had Velcro flaps. *Brendan couldn't tie his shoelaces anymore.*

He looked up, saw me watching him. "I *like* these shoes."

An image flashed into my mind: Brendan's swimming stroke as he powered across the lake on a summer morning. Now he couldn't tie his own shoes. I ached for him. Brendan knew what was in store for him: the pain, the sickening aftereffects, the very real possibility that he would die.

I put my arms around him. "This is going to work out," I said. It had to.

Less than twenty minutes later, Brendan and I stepped out of the hotel into hazy morning light. He stood quietly, resting an arm on the roof of the car, and he still *looked* healthy. He was taking in a coffee shop's blinking neon sign, then a field-stone church across the street, as if he were memorizing each mundane detail.

"Pretty diner, pretty church, *very* pretty girl," he said. Then he climbed into the passenger seat. A little stiffly. I heard the seat belt click as Brendan strapped in for the ride of his life.

"Let's go, beautiful. We have an appointment in Samarra or someplace like that."

For one of the only times that summer, the two of us were mostly quiet. The early-morning drive took only a few minutes from the Colonial to the St. Marys underground garage. An elevator took us up to the first floor. From there, we headed along a stained-glass corridor to the Joseph Building, which was where Brendan would be admitted and prepped for surgery.

Brendan stopped and put his hands on top of my shoulders. He leaned in and held me and stared into my eyes.

"I think that I've run out of jokes, Jennifer. Do you mind if I tell you that I love you again?"

"No. Please." *Just keep talking. Don't leave me.*

"I love you so much, Jennifer. It's important to me that whatever happens, you know you did great, fabulous. You helped me be strong, more than you know. You did everything that anyone could do, and then some. . . . *Jennifer?*"

"I know," I finally said. "I got it." I held him even tighter. My eyes squeezed shut, but tears were rolling down my cheeks anyway.

"You're letting me cry," I finally managed to say.

"Uh-huh. Yeah. That's because I am, too."

I looked into his eyes and saw that he was almost as big a mess as I was. Brendan leaned forward and kissed me on the cheeks, then my eyes, finally my lips. I loved the way he kissed, loved everything about him. I didn't want to let him go.

"There's never enough time, is there?" he said. "I think I have to go. I'm late, Jennifer."

Once we arrived on the fifth floor, the admissions nurse, a portly woman with strong freckled arms, sorted through a pile of papers. Then she called for an orderly, who appeared with a wheelchair. That's when the thought I really hadn't been able to face flooded my mind. *I might never see Brendan again. This could be it.*

"I love you," I said. "I'll be waiting right here. I'll be waiting where I'm standing now."

Brendan said, "I love you, Jennifer. Who wouldn't love the most beautiful girl in the world? One way or the other, I will see you."

He smiled that wonderful smile of his and gave me a double thumbs-up as the orderly wheeled him down the long hallway to surgery. Then Brendan let loose with one of his famous go-jump-in-the-lake screams.

I clapped my hands together and laughed. "Bye," I called. "Bye."

Brendan looked back, smiled again.

Just before he disappeared, he yelled, "Byc!"

Seventy

~

BYE?

Don't let it be bye.

I slid down into an upholstered chair in the corner of the hospital waiting room and began to imagine the operation going on six floors below me when Shep arrived with Brendan's mother and father, whom I had never met.

"He didn't want us to come," said Mrs. Keller. "He's trying to make it easier for us. Or so he thinks."

"He's always been that way," said Brendan's father. "He broke his hand once in high school and didn't tell us until it was nearly healed. I'm Andrew, by the way. This is Eileen."

We all hugged. Then Brendan's mother and father went straight to tears. I could see how much they loved their son, and it touched me.

The rest of the day crept by at an excruciatingly slow pace. I glanced down at Brendan's watch every few minutes, and the hands almost didn't seem to move. Brendan's father told jokes, which wasn't much of a surprise. My favorite was, "How do you recognize an extrovert computer geek? He looks at *your* shoes."

Other visitors drifted in and out of the waiting room, a few of them crying, most looking worried. The television flickered with never-ending images of the news, CNBC, ESPN.

As we waited I wondered if Shep might be Doc. But he hadn't raised his children alone. So he *wasn't* Doc — unless Sam had pulled a fast one.

At about four I left the waiting-around room for a while. I wandered down to the Peace Garden in the St. Marys compound, a square filled with bright flowers and a statue of Saint Francis. I heard a carillon concert, the bells ringing out a pretty rendition of "Amazing Grace." I got down on my knees and prayed for Brendan. Then I called Sam and told her about the day so far.

Finally I returned to the waiting room. My timing was excellent. Ten hours after I had kissed Brendan good-bye, a young doctor with dark hair and a cherubic face appeared. He announced that he was Adam Kolski. He didn't look old enough to be a surgeon, let alone "practically a goddddd."

I tried to read his face, but my journalistic skills weren't working very well that day.

"Things went as well as could be expected," Dr. Kolski said. "Brendan survived the surgery."

Seventy-one

~

VISITORS were permitted to see patients in the ICU for just a few minutes. One person at a time. After the Kellers and Shep took their turn, I went in. Adam Kolski came along with me to check on his patient. "He's doing better than he looks," Kolski warned.

Brendan was unconscious. His head was swaddled in bandages, and his face was black and blue. Dr. Kolski explained that Brendan had been tubed and that machines could keep him alive, just in case.

There was a tube in Brendan's nose, another in his throat; a catheter led to a bag under the bed; and IV towers dripped saline and sedatives into his veins. Electrodes were stuck all over him, sending reports on his vital signs to several monitors; a blood pressure cuff on one arm inflated and deflated automatically.

"He's alive," I whispered. "That's the only important thing."

"He is alive," Dr. Kolski said, and patted my shoulder. "He did this for you, Jennifer. He told me that you're worth it and more. Talk to him. You might be the medicine Brendan needs right now."

Then Kolski stepped out of the room and I was alone with Brendan. I took off the watch he'd given me and gently buckled it over his wrist, right next to the plastic bracelet with his name on it. I squeezed Brendan's fingers and leaned close to his face.

"I'm right here," I said, willing him to hear my voice. "You know, I've loved every minute I've spent with you this summer. *But especially this one.*"

Seventy-two

~

IT SEEMED as though my precious five minutes with Brendan was over in about five seconds. I was holding his hand, and then I was pulled away by a polite but firm nurse who sent me reeling out to the waiting room again.

Mr. and Mrs. Keller and Shep wanted to take me to dinner, but I was emotionally and physically wasted. I couldn't leave Brendan right then. When they left, I sank into a chair and let the tears sheet down my cheeks. I had restrained myself most of the day, but now I had no reason to hold back. All kinds of thoughts and voices were inside my head. *Brendan could die soon.* Well-meaning people would say, "Jennifer, you're still young. Grieve, but you have to move on. Don't shut out love."

I wasn't — *I loved Brendan!* I hadn't shut out love, but look where it had gotten me. I mopped my face with tissues, then stared at the empty rows of chairs lit by harsh white light. Outside the window, the street whined with a thin stream of traffic whizzing past. I felt so alone at the hospital.

The minutes passed slowly. Eventually an hour went by. I would have called Sam again, but it was too late.

I finally dug into my handbag and lifted out the last packet of her letters. I untied the frayed red string and fanned out the envelopes. My name danced across the length of them in her clear and distinct hand.

I bought a cup of coffee from the machine, stirred in several packets of sugar.

Then I pried open an envelope flap. "I need to hear your voice, Sam," I said.

In the endless white night of the hospital waiting room, I began to read the end of Sam's story.

Seventy-three

Dear Jen,

Here's what happened — everything changed in an instant.

Doc knocked on my kitchen door one pathetically hot day in August, and the moment I saw him, my heart started banging around in my chest. I was stunned and maybe even scared. Jennifer, he had never been to my house like that before.

"Is something the matter?" I asked. "Are you all right? What's happened?"

All he said was "Come take a ride with me."

"Right now? Like this?"

"Yep. You look just fine, Samantha. I've got a surprise for you."

"A good surprise?"

"The best I could come up with. I've been waiting a long time for this one."

Whatever he was up to, I was having none of it in my dirt-stained overalls and gardening clogs. So I let him inside the house and went upstairs to change. Fifteen minutes later I was wearing a pretty blue linen dress, my hair was neat, and I'd even put on some lipstick.

When he saw me, Doc smiled. "God, you're gorgeous," he said. Of course, he would think I was gorgeous if I were wearing a trash bag with a tuna casserole on my head. I told him so, and we both laughed, because it was true.

And then he grabbed both my hands. "Samantha, everything changes today."

"And you're not going to tell me *what* changes today?" I asked.

"No, I want to show you."

He wasn't just enthusiastic, he was very mysterious, Jen, which added to the fun. Of course, I was excited just to see him, to look into his face and see how happy he was.

And you know what? I really do like surprises!

Seventy-four

~

Jennifer, Jennifer, Jennifer,
That whole week the Venetian Festival
had been going full blast in the village, and
the streets were mobbed with tourists
who'd come to the annual end-of-summer
bash at the lake. Doc parked in a munici-
pal lot a block north of Main Street and
fed a pocket full of quarters into the meter.
It seemed that we were going to the fair,
and apparently we would be staying for a
while.

"Is this your surprise?" I asked. "Because I kind of knew the festival was in
town."

287

"This is just the venue," he said. "Don't be such a wisenheimer." Which was one of Doc's favorite words, if it even is a word.

Kids were screaming on the roller coaster, the air smelled of buttered popcorn and cotton candy, and it suddenly struck me that I was in a moment I thought would never come. There we were, Doc and I walking hand in hand together in downtown Lake Geneva. I looked up at him with a big question written across my face. "Is this your surprise? Because it's a great one, actually. Are we out of the closet?"

Doc told me that he had just dropped his youngest off at Vanderbilt University. "The nest is empty. No more Mr. Mom," he said. "I'm free."

Suddenly Doc pulled me into his arms and kissed me in front of God and everybody else in Lake Geneva. His kiss was so full of love that tears popped out of my eyes.

He looked into my eyes. "I wonder if

anybody has ever had a love affair like ours, Samantha. You know, I doubt it."

"That's part of what makes it special, I guess."

The sun was warm on my face, the air was cool, and as I swayed in Doc's arms, I felt alive in a way I never had before. This was even better than our weekends to Copper Harbor because for the first time we were absolutely free. I was *flying,* Jennifer, but somehow my feet were still on the ground as we reached Library Park.

We found an empty bench next to the seawall. We watched the *Lady of the Lake* cast off from the Riviera Docks, and Doc bought hot dogs and beers from the Veterans' stand. We stayed way after the sun went down, watching the lit boat parade and the fireworks finale.

And here's the amazing thing. It would be insulting if it weren't so funny. During that whole day Doc and I spoke with people we knew, and not one of them noticed that we were glowing. I got it, of course. People just couldn't conceive of romance between the two of us. How strange and backwards the world can be sometimes. So many people just give up on love, even though love is the best thing that can happen to them.

I turned to Doc and told him how much I loved him and that I couldn't imagine a better surprise. He pulled me close. "Brace yourself, Samantha. Our day isn't over."

Seventy-five

~

Doc's car purred contentedly as we drove away from the festival, past the outskirts of town. I didn't have a clue what was going on. Not until we pulled into the lot of the Yerkes Observatory. It was quiet, and all I could hear were the chirping of crickets and maybe my own pulse beating in my ears.

Doc grabbed a plaid blanket from the backseat, and as we'd done years before, we ran on tiptoes across the lawn fronting the imposing building. A pal of Doc's had left a key for us in a crack between two bricks in the wall. We climbed the three flights of stairs to the largest dome and entered into darkness.

"Are you ready for this?" he asked.

I smiled and felt open to just about anything. "I've been ready for years."

He used a penlight to find a lever that actually lifted the floor until it sat still about five feet below the eyepiece of the telescope. Then he operated the cranks and winches that opened the dome revealing a wide swath of sky.

"Look at that, Samantha. Just look at it. It's heaven."

"Oh my God" was all I could manage to say at that moment, because I was spellbound.

Doc stood close behind me with his hands on my shoulders as we peered through the world's largest refracting lens. It did seem as if we were looking at heaven. The sky was bedazzling, to say the least. I didn't know what to gaze at first, but my eye was drawn to a dappled red globe the size of a silver dollar.

"That's Mars," said Doc.

Doc told me that Mars and Earth were in opposition that night, lined up in their orbits so that Earth was between Mars and the sun. He pointed out polar ice caps, dark smudges called limb haze, and what might have been a dust storm blowing across the face of the planet under its misty pink sky.

"The last time Mars was this close to Earth, cavemen were freezing their buns off in New Guinea, hoping someone would discover fire," he said.

Next Doc spread the blanket on the hardwood floor and led me to it. We sat down, shoulder to shoulder. I knew something good was coming, but I had no idea what it could be. "What?" I whispered.

"I've been waiting for just the right moment," he said. "You did say that you liked surprises, Samantha."

Seventy-six

"Samantha, I am such a lucky person,"
Doc said in the softest voice. "I found
you a little late, but I love you more than
anything else on this earth, and here you
are in my arms. You are absolutely my best
friend, my soul mate, my confidante, my
sweet, sweet love. I don't like it at all
when you're not around. I still can't
believe that I found you, or you found me,
at that awful Red Cross dinner dance. I
really can't, Samantha — and now here
we are."

I still didn't know where this was going,
but my heart was starting to beat uncon-
trollably. Ever since I had known him,

Doc had always told me, quite beautifully sometimes, how he felt about me, but that night was even more special, more passionate, more touching, and sweeter — which, in my opinion, is a good thing. He showed me a small box, and I shone the penlight onto it.

"Open it," he said.

I did, and my eyes widened immediately. Inside was a sapphire ring surrounded by small, gorgeous diamonds. It took my breath away, and not for the reason you think. Years before — *once* — I had pointed out this very piece in Tiffany's in Chicago. I had loved it then, but now it brought tears to my eyes. I couldn't believe Doc had remembered and was giving it to me.

He slid it onto my finger, then said, "I love you dearly, more than anything. . . . Will you marry me, Samantha?"

My eyes were so wide with wonder, Jennifer. Doc's face was framed by the sky and the stars above. I put my arms around him and held tight. I honestly had never expected this, never dared to think it could happen.

I could barely speak. "I love *you* more than anything, too. I'm so lucky I found you. Of course I'll marry you. I'd be a fool not to."

And then I said Doc's real name, over and over again, as the stars looked down on the two of us, and everything seemed pretty darn good with the universe.

Seventy-seven

~

I HAD FALLEN asleep after reading Sam's last amazing letter. But, boy, did I have questions to ask her when I got back to Lake Geneva. Or maybe even when I called her again from the hotel. Why hadn't she married Doc? What had happened to them?

I awoke to someone gently shaking my arm, calling my name. Morning light filtered through the plate-glass window of the waiting room. Adam Kolski hovered over me.

"Good morning, Jennifer. We could have gotten a more comfortable place for you to sleep," he said.

"Is everything all right with Brendan?" I asked immediately.

"He slept through the night, just like you. No promises, but he can move his toes," the doctor said. "He knows his name, and he knows yours. Actually, he's asking for you."

That perked me right up. "Can I see him?"

"Of course. That's why I came to get you. I want you to talk to Brendan. I need to find out if he really knows you. Come with me."

Kolski, the goddddd himself, opened the sliding doors to Brendan's small room in the ICU. "Just five minutes," he said.

I could see Brendan behind Dr. Kolski as I eased myself into the room. There was a rolled-up washcloth in his right hand. I took it away and slipped my hand inside his.

"It's Jennifer," I whispered. "Ready for our morning swim in the lake?"

There wasn't any response from Brendan, which didn't surprise me but also didn't make me feel reassured about his condition. I had no idea how much damage had been done during the operation.

"I'm here. I just wanted you to know. And *you're* here, too."

I was babbling a little but I didn't care, and I doubted that it would make much difference to Brendan. If he could even recognize my voice.

Then, as I stood by his bed, a miracle happened, or so it seemed to me. Brendan squeezed my hand, the slightest pressure, but it sent shivers through my body. I lowered my head. "I'm right here, Brendan. Don't try to talk. I'll talk for both of us. I'm here, sweetheart."

"Are you real?"

My head shot up and I looked at Brendan again. My God, *he had talked*.

"I'm here," I said, my voice cracking with unbelievable emotion. *Brendan had talked.* "Can you feel my hand? That's me squeezing."

"I can't see you," he said in a hoarse whisper.

"That's because your eyes are swollen shut."

He was silent for a long moment, and I thought maybe he'd fallen back asleep.

"I didn't think . . . I'd make it," Brendan said at last.

I could see he was trying hard not to cry, but then tears leaked out of his tightly closed eyes. "We're going to be okay," he said.

Suddenly I was seized with such an overpowering feeling of humility, but also love for this man. Brendan was reassuring *me.* He was there for me, even now, after his terrible operation. His voice was kind of faraway, but it was Brendan, definitely my boy. And he wanted to talk. "I was thinking . . . you sitting on the dock . . . shielding sun from your eyes . . . looking at me . . . I held that thought."

I looked at Brendan's face, loving him so much. And then another miracle happened. His eyes opened to slits. And he struggled to make a cracked, semidrugged smile.

It was only the best smile I'd ever seen in my life.

"I love you so much," I whispered. "Oh my God, do I love you."

"Don't fight me on this . . . I love you more."

And at that moment I understood something that had seemed impossible — Brendan was going to live.

Seventy-eight

~

DURING THE NEXT few weeks every-thing in life seemed incredibly precious and had more meaning for me. Suddenly I was a regular at the Mayo Clinic and Lake-land Medical Center in Lake Geneva. All I was missing was a candy striper's outfit.

Brendan's recuperation was slow and excruciating, but he kept getting a little stronger every day, week after week. He was a favorite with his therapist, partly be-cause he wore a different goofy hat every day, partly because he went three weeks without letting them know he was a high and mighty doctor, but mostly because he has such endearing ways.

And then one rainy morning in October, we were summoned to Adam Kolski's office in the St. Marys building. The godddd showed us some X-rays, then abruptly told Brendan that he could go home. He was in remission.

"You can go home, too, Jennifer," Kolski said, and offered a rare smile.

The next day Brendan and I set sail for Lake Geneva. On the way to Wisconsin, I was jumpy with excitement and maybe even a little case of the nerves. We were going to see Sam. She was back at her house, and there was something else. When I called and told her the news about Brendan, Sam said she wanted us to meet Doc.

Early October was a time of year I had never loved, because the sun drops below the horizon a little earlier every afternoon. But I was happy to see this particular October. I had so much to be thankful for. Brendan and Sam, and now I would get to meet Doc.

And then there was Sam's house — straight ahead. I could see Henry's old pickup parked by the garden. Hmmm.

Brendan climbed out of the Jaguar and took a deep breath of lake air. I called out in a loud voice, "Sam! We're here. You have company."

Then Brendan let loose with one of his whoops — not quite the usual volume but noisy enough to scare some bluebirds from overhanging tree branches.

"Race you to the lake?" he said, and grinned. I knew he was still a little weak, but he looked good and his famous smile was working just fine.

When Sam didn't answer, I slipped into the dark of the house to look for her. I called her name in every room I came to, my voice rising as my footsteps rang out on the hardwood floors. Fear came over me a little too quickly those days. Too many bad things had happened, or maybe it was that lately things had been going too well.

"Jen," I heard Brendan call from the porch. "She's out here. Sam's down by the lake."

Heart booming, with an almost girlish delight, I rattled down the stairs again, then burst out the back of the house. I saw that Sam had set up chairs under the shade tree — and she wasn't alone.

A man sat beside her in the shadows. He was wearing a golden ball cap with a V, probably Vanderbilt, which made all the sense in the world suddenly.

"Doc," I said under my breath. "I should have known."

Seventy-nine

~

I HURRIED down the sloping lawn as fast as I could go, right into Sam's outstretched arms. It felt so right to be there again. A moment later Sam moved over to Brendan and gave him a long hug. It was as if they'd been best friends for life.

Then she turned toward the man of her dreams. "I'd like you to meet Doc," she said to me. And to Brendan, "This is John Farley. He is a doctor, actually. In philosophy, from the Vanderbilt School of Divinity. Everything is coming together beautifully, Jennifer. Life does that sometimes."

My God, the Reverend John Farley was Doc, and he and Sam were such a handsome couple. I loved seeing them together like that. It just made my heart sing.

The four of us settled in under the shifting shade of an old maple tree. I said, "Wow," and my mouth kept stretching into grins as I watched Sam and Doc — John — exchange touches and glances.

I hugged Brendan, and he whispered in my ear, "I agree — *wow*."

Everything *was* coming together pretty well, I had to admit. A while later the four of us were cluttering up Sam's kitchen. Doc peeled potatoes in maddeningly thin, unbroken curls. Brendan alternated between shelling peas and eating them. I was getting flour all over everything.

Until Sam finally said, "Everyone out of my kitchen. Leave the cooking to the professionals!" We laughed and moved the party out to the dining room. Forty minutes later we helped Sam put the meal on the table. Roast beef, sweet potatoes, onions and peas, homemade biscuits.

Over dinner I asked John Farley a

question that I had been saving up. "You asked Samantha to marry you. Sam, you said you'd be a fool not to." I looked from Sam's face to his. "So what happened?"

Sam looked at Doc. "Well, I talked her into it; then I talked her out of it," he said.

Sam laughed. "He just raised some good questions and issues. Like the fact of life that some busybodies around town would have questions, and opinions, and *judgments*. They'd make jokes about the two of us being *The Thorn Birds*. I didn't think I'd like that so much. We were too used to our privacy. It also might be hurtful to John's congregation. Then he had a really good idea."

He tilted his head at Sam. "I said, what if we didn't tell anyone? What if we keep our love between the two of us? We talked about it, and that's what we decided to do. Everything about us had always been different anyway."

Sam reached over and took John's hand in hers. "Doc and I were married on a

Sunday in August two years ago, in Copper Harbor, Michigan. No one knows that, except the two of you."

We clinked glasses around the table. "To Samantha and Doc!" Brendan and I said.

"To Brendan and Jennifer!" they said.

Sam gave me another big hug, and so did Doc. They both hugged Brendan. Then we sat around exchanging stories for the next couple of hours. We watched darkness come over the lake, and Doc told us about the stars, and I doubt that Stephen Hawking could have done a better job. I was so happy, and I remember every moment of that night in Lake Geneva. I always will.

Because less than three weeks later, something really terrible happened.

Eighty

~

IN SAM'S WORDS, *life works like that sometimes.*

Early in November I sat on the old blue velvet sofa in Sam's living room. Brendan held one of my hands, and Doc held the other. "It will be all right," Doc whispered, touching his chest with a shaking hand. "She's safe inside us. Sam is at peace."

Every minute or so, an umbrella would tip-tap the porch floorboards, then the front door would whine open and another of Sam's friends would blow in on a damp gust of wind. Soon the house was filled with people from Lake Geneva and Chicago and even Copper Harbor, all looking uncomfortable to find themselves there on that unthinkable occasion.

As I looked around, I could see intimations of Sam everywhere.

In my cousin Bobby's baby blue eyes, in the clusters of family photos on the walls, on my aunt Val's tear-streaked face as she stared out the picture window to the broken surface of a rain-swept lake. It was so sad, and almost unbelievable that the person who had drawn so many people together in life wasn't there with us.

Finally Doc leaned in close. "If you're ready, I think we should start. Samantha wouldn't want to keep everybody waiting. We shouldn't, either."

As Doc began to speak about his Samantha — though still not revealing their incredible secret — I pressed the side of my face into Brendan's shoulder. Doc was so brave up there, so eloquent, and more touching than anyone else in the room knew. Meanwhile, the deaths of other people I'd loved flashed through my mind:

Grandpa Charles, my mother, Danny. Brendan gently held mc, and I listened to Doc and then Sam's other friends, each telling a cherished story or remembrance.

Then there was a lull, and Brendan finally whispered, "Go ahead, Jen. It's your turn."

Eighty-one

~

I DON'T LIKE public speaking or being
the center of attention, but I felt that I had
to get up and talk. This was my grandmother, my Sam. I experienced the light-
headedness that comes just before you
faint as I walked to the front of the room.

I stood with my back to the lake, a favorite black-and-white photograph of Sam
to my right. I looked out at all the sad
yet expectant eyes of my grandmother's
friends. Brendan smiled encouragement.
Doc winked, and a calm finally came over
me.

This is what I said:

"Please bear with me. I'm not good at

313

this, but there are things I have to say. When I was growing up, I spent my precious summer vacations in this house with Grandma Sam."

I started to choke up the first time I said her name. Then I didn't care if I was crying, and I surged forward.

"The two of us were best friends right from the start. We just clicked, had chemistry, shared a worldview, laughed and cried at the same things. I loved her more than anyone, and I admired her so much.

"I always told her my most private thoughts when we were in bed: Sam sitting beside me, her hand over mine in the dark. Some kids are afraid of the dark, but I loved it, at least when I was with Sam.

"It feels a little like that, now. I can't see Sam, but I know she's here.

"Not too long ago, I had retreated from life because, well, I think I couldn't stand the pain of living fully. It was Sam who gently coaxed me out of my shell and removed my veil of sadness. It was Sam who showed me the way to find love again. Sam led me to Brendan, whom I love dearly.

"But there is a secret that I never got to share with Sam, so I'll tell her now. Sam, dear — Samantha — I have something wonderful to tell you. Brendan and I are going to have a baby. Your first great-grandchild."

Then I did start crying, but I knew I was smiling, too. I looked right at Doc, and he was beaming. So was Brendan.

"Can't you all just see Sam's face? The way it lights up, the way Sam *listens,* as if you're the most important person in the world?

"Right now, I almost can't believe that she will never see our baby, that she won't find a way somehow.

"But I also wonder if he or she will have Sam's beautiful curls. Or those sparkling blue eyes, or her amazing ability to love so many people, to have such great friends. But *this* is for sure. Our child will know all about his or her great-grandmother, what an incredible person she was. I have all of Sam's stories to tell. I know exactly who my grandmother was, and that's such a treasure.

"And boy or girl, no matter what, our baby's name will be *Sam*."

Eighty-two

~

SAM'S FRIENDS and the family told stories about her for hours that afternoon; some close friends, and some not so close, stayed late into the night, and every story seemed a little better than the one before. Of course, I had more stories than anyone else. I had Sam's letters. I just couldn't tell anybody too much of what I knew. That was a secret among Doc, Brendan, and me.

Brendan's uncle came up to me before he left for the night. Shep leaned in and kissed me on the cheek. "I wanted to wait until it quieted down some," he said. "You did so great today, Jennifer. I loved what you said about your grandmother. Sam wanted

317

you to have this. I've been keeping it for you at the law office."

I took a white linen envelope from Shep. Was it one more of her letters? What did she have to tell me now? Another dark secret?

I slid my finger under the envelope flap. Then I took out a single page and began to read.

Dearest Jennifer,

I guess this is our last talk, and don't you dare be sad. That was never our style. When your grandfather and I bought the lake house fifty years ago, it was a fixer-upper on stony soil, but it had the most gorgeous views of the lake. I have so many glorious memories of this place, and so do you. I can still see you and your mother curled up on the couch in front of the fire while I cooked one of my dinners. Valerie gave birth to Bobby upstairs in the east bedroom, and both you and your cousin left permanent ice skate tracks on the kitchen floor. (Of course, I *knew* you did it.) I remember all the summers we spent on the front porch, but most of all, I remember the times I've had with you, Jennifer. You were always "my best."

I'm looking out across the lake now as I write. Winter will be here before long; the branches will glisten with ice, and snow will blow across the lake like a fine lace curtain. I can't wait for that to happen.

But I am also already looking forward to spring. The freshly painted docks will go back into the lake, the garden will shake off the snow, and the perennials will reemerge. And what I'm thinking is that the word *perennial* is a misnomer. *Long-lived* might be more correct, because perennials don't live forever. Not even sassy ones like me. This is why I'm preparing for the future, today.

Of course, I'm taking care of everyone I love, but I have a special gift for you. Actually, it's *inside* the envelope with this letter. Use it well — I know you will.

Jennifer, my heart is full, and my life has been, too. That's a great thing. I have my Doc. I have you, and you have Brendan. I couldn't be any happier. What more could anyone ask for?

All my love, and remember — *you are my best friend, you are "my best."*

Sam

A small weight shifted inside the envelope, which sent it floating from my hand. I bent to retrieve the envelope, and a brass key tied to a round cardboard tag with a frayed red string slid out.

I picked up the key and looked at the tag.

On one side, Sam had written: *23 Knollwood Road, the house is yours now, Jennifer.*

On the other side was a short inscription. I looked at what Sam had written. Her last words to me, ever.

Love never dies.

EPILOGUE

Pictures for Sam

Eighty-three

~

BRENDAN AND I arrange ourselves on the couch in front of the handy-dandy, state-of-the-art Sony video camera, which is set up and ready for our very first home movie.

We're in our new Chicago apartment, with its view of Lake Michigan, and we're as excited as can be. This is an important moment in our lives, seminal stuff. At least, we seem to think so.

"You ready? Okay, I'll turn it on," Brendan says, then jumps up and switches on the video camera. He is full of life these days — in remission — like the rest of us, right?

"You start, Jen," he says. "You're never at a loss for words."

"Hello, Samantha," I say, and grin like a fool and finger-wave to the camera. "It's Mommy, when she was thirty-five and not afraid to tell her age."

Brendan is leaning in beside me. "And I'm your proud, very happy dad, as of fourteen days and about eleven hours."

"We love you very, very much, sweetheart, and a couple of times a year —"

"Maybe more than a couple," Brendan says. "See, your mom and dad are frustrated actors. Obviously, we're windbags, too."

I say, "We're going to film ourselves and try to give you an idea of who we are, what we're like, what we're thinking about, and, of course, how much we love you."

I look at Brendan and he picks up the thread, which we have semirehearsed.

"So that when you get old and infirm like the two of us — or me, anyway — you'll be able to look at these tapes and know who we were. Is that cool?"

"And how *silly* we were. . . . But also how much we treasure having you as our daughter. Right now, you're sleeping, and you're a very, very good sleeper."

Brendan starts to clap, and also lets Sam see his movie-star smile. "Hooray! Good going, Samantha. Keep it up! You go, girl! Way to sleep!"

I say, "Samantha, you have the most beautiful blue eyes, a breathtaking smile, like your dad — and neither of us can get enough of you."

"You're also bald as a cue ball, but Mama dresses you in pink so we know you're a girly girl," Brendan teases, but sweetly, as is his way.

"Here's an interesting tidbit," I say. "When you were born, at the moment you appeared in the world, you looked around like a curious little bird peeking out for the first time from its nest. You looked right at me, checked me out — and then you looked at your dad, checked him out — and then you smiled gloriously at both of us. Now, supposedly, according to the doctor in the house, you couldn't possibly smile or see us yet, but we don't believe that."

"I'm the doctor, and I don't believe it," says Brendan. "Did I mention that you're bald as an egg?"

"You did," I say. "Now let us start at the very beginning of this wonderful story, the start of it all, Samantha. Let me tell you how you got your name. It's a beautiful name and an even more beautiful story. And you, Sam, are its happy ending."

And then I am silent for a moment, and I don't say this, but I am thinking, *Love never dies, Sam.*

About the Author

James Patterson is the author of the ac-
claimed Alex Cross and Women's Murder
Club series. His love story *Suzanne's Diary
for Nicholas* was a runaway success and
his top bestseller. He lives in Florida.

3 1489 00504 9257

so   Patterson, James.

Sam's letters to
Jennifer.

DATE			

24.95   7-02-04

FREEPORT MEMORIAL LIBRARY
144 W. Merrick Rd.
Freeport, N.Y. 11520

FREEPORT MEMORIAL LIBRARY

BAKER & TAYLOR